W9-ATN-694

RISING

RISING

DARNELLA FORD

St. Martin's Griffin ✢ New York

ISBN 0-7394-3243-5

I dedicate this book to the *survivor* because you could have split in two because the pain was so great. And dissolved into nothing because the hurt ran so deep. And disappeared without a fight or a breath or a hope or a reason to ever wake up again but you didn't.

You are the reason I wrote this story.

ACKNOWLEDGMENTS

Before I utter a sound I must tell you that *this* story blew holes in my heart as I wrote it. And though this work is purely fiction, it is as real as you and I.

I would imagine that every artist hopes to make a profound statement to the world through his or her art, and I find myself wishing for no different.

All of my life I have dreamt of waking up in a world where I would one day be allowed to project my voice beyond the confines of my own head. *I now live in that world.* And to that end I would like to acknowledge and salute the visionary who first found the story and then diligently searched to find the author of it, me. Monique Patterson, you are the bomb! I thank you for caring about this project enough to give your own blood for it. It is because of your faith I am able to say I believe in destiny *again*. And to St. Martin's Press, you have been a kind and gracious host. I thank you most of all for giving my voice an ECHO.

To my agent, Claudia Menza, *thank you* for believing in me before there was even a reason to believe. You came along during a time in my life when I desperately needed a cosigner for this dream.

Special acknowledgment to my daughter, Morgan. You are the reason I show up every day and do this thing called *life*. My wish for you is simple, that your childhood be a smashing success and not something you spend the rest of your life trying to get *over*. You are my best friend and the only walking miracle I have ever known.

To my parents, John and Corliss, thank you for breathing me into existence. Especially to my mother, for graciously helping me organize all of the chatter inside of my head. To my four sisters, Kimberly, Franyaro, Monique, and LaShawna—in each of your hearts I see the best of who I can be.

To my grandmother, Nana, even though you left before I was ready to let you go, your unconditional love remains to date the most beautiful symphony I have ever heard.

To Michael, Patty, and Grandma Boo, I thank you because you have given me one of the greatest gifts there is: you have loved my child as though she were your own. I would like also to give a special acknowledgment to Thomas Hughes Jr., because your love for Morgan gives me gentle confirmation that the human race may not be damned after all.

To my family at Epsteen and Associates, thank you for your support of this ridiculous dream to live a life less ordinary. Especially to Michael, thank you for being my father during the times in my life when I so desperately needed to be *somebody's* child.

And to the angels who took on the form of man and came

into my life as my friends and soul mates—Natasha Munson, Barbara Hansen, Sharon Pheghley, Goldie Jordane, Jernicca Claville, Betty Singh, and M. J. Steele—your unconditional love and friendship is the strongest confirmation that I have truly *lived*.

And last but certainly not least, my list of acknowledgments would not be complete if I neglected to inscribe my eternal gratitude to the Creator of the heavens and the Earth for the majesty of language. My fascination and obsession for the manipulation of words has led me to take on the erratic journey of the writer. Thank you, Father. I shall always be grateful for *the gift*.

BY the time
the cut scabbed
and the bump healed
and the bruise disappeared
and the welt went down
and the tears dried
and the dent unbent
and the scars smoothed
and the discoloration blended
and the anger quieted
and the violence aged to weakness
and the fear retired
I was dangling from the wings of insanity.
And no matter how hard I tried
To keep my crack concealed
On any given day
On every given day
From the bottom of my feet
To the top of my head
I could feel insanity RISING.

RISING

PROLOGUE

The dark and I were bitter enemies. It was never welcome in my world. Defined as the opposite of light, the dark was so much more. It was my prison, and I, its captive. I was held hostage by its embrace and this irrational fear dictated how I moved about my everyday life.

I was paranoid of dark corners, absolutely crippled by them. I did not frequent movie theaters or auditoriums, nor did I patronize dark coffeehouses. I didn't go *anywhere* I couldn't *stay* till morning should I get caught against the horizon's backside and find myself on the flip side of daylight.

My one-bedroom loft boasted of thirty-nine lights.

Nightlights. Daylights. Flashlights. Stoplights. And Bud Lites. Every one of them lit up on command.

I had a hundred and thirteen lightbulbs in my cupboard on

standby. After a major blackout in the summer of '96, I went as far as to spend seven thousand dollars on a couch that glowed in the dark.

I didn't do it because I was crazy or half-cocked. I think it would be presumptuous of you to classify me as unstable, repressed, or psychotic.

I don't particularly care for therapy because I only end up sleeping with the therapist before the sessions are concluded.

I've never gotten off on Prozac, and Valium messes with my head. I don't do cocaine or heroin, and methamphetamines give me the runs.

I hate Aristotle because he was a know-it-all and I take great offense at your third-rate advice because you're probably just as disturbed as me.

Not that I'm "batty" at all, I remind you. And though you've probably condemned me as "crazy," I think you'll find I'm saner than you'd like me to be.

Every word I write has meaning.

I don't babble because I like to stare at the contrast of black ink against white pages. And I'm certainly not telling this story to blow a sunny breeze of entertainment up your other end. I wrote this story because I want you to know why the dark was my enemy.

In the dark I was easy prey for the Beast. The blackness of night rendered me helpless. Pain radiates as I recall the brief but frequent encounters. Sharp, splintered aches cut through bone as I stand by helplessly and watch my flesh literally crawl when I remember.

I associate darkness with the Beast. Darkness was where the Beast danced naked, his clammy skin against mine. He slithered like a vile animal claiming victims without conscience.

He stole innocence without permission and his savagery left

dents in my soul. Even when he wasn't around I smelled him, a tropical musty funk. His flesh generated a cryptic odor, an ambiguous mark of his presence.

I remember the nights I danced with the Beast. They were unforgettable nights I shall spend the rest of my life trying to forget.

The Beast couldn't be tracked because he didn't have an address. You couldn't knock on his door because he didn't want to be found. You couldn't call him at home for comment and God knows he would never take responsibility for his squalor. He would deny his existence if challenged, and could change form right before your eyes.

Colorless.

Weightless.

Nameless.

Timeless.

And yes, at twenty-seven years old, I knew he was as real as the darkness that kept me from shutting my eyes all the way at night.

PART ONE

CHAPTER ONE

My name is Symone. And more important than my name is my story and the unveiling of the Beast.

I was adopted.

My adoptive parents were the Hustons, a shameless family with a house at the top of the hill.

The Huston name was synonymous with class, power, and money. Ridge Huston specialized in international trade. He made money because he had money. He didn't work much, but he didn't have to. He owned *everything* and it worked for him.

Madeline was his wife but I referred to her as the "other hand" that dipped into the cash. She led a life of leisure with no grand responsibilities, unless someone counted the children she had borne him. And even those obligations were oftentimes dictated to working stiffs known as nannies.

The Hustons were one of Eden's most prominent and well respected families. They weren't respected because they were deserving of respect. They were respected because they had money.

Big difference.

Ridge and Madeline adopted me when I was nine. And that was the turning point of my life. They rescued me from the inner city of Dorchester, Massachusetts, and swept me away to Michigan's most pretentious community of Eden.

Eden was an asymmetric paradise and just because it was upscale didn't mean it was also upstanding. The hillside homes hung million-dollar price tags off their front doors.

It was prestigious and downright uppity.

In that city, even dog shit could be packaged and sold as a souvenir. But only if the shit belonged to an Eden household pet. And everybody knew that an animal residing in Eden was worth more than a human living in the city.

The life the Hustons introduced me to was much different than the one I knew so intimately as a child.

In Dorchester, I had slept on a pee-stained cot in a single-room dump. We were economically challenged. Translation: dirt-poor.

We had been strangers to the conveniences of the telephone, heated water, or an abundant food supply.

We had eaten toasted bread for breakfast, plain bread for lunch, and cheese bread for dinner.

In the ghetto, tap water was an all-you-could-drink commodity. The only catch: Your teeth would turn yellow if you drank too much.

Every month was a hustle just to pay rent. I worried that if it wasn't paid by the fifteenth, we'd be out bargaining with the bum on the corner, trading a slice of cheese bread for deluxe accommodations in one of his finest cardboard boxes.

RISING

Did I neglect to mention Dolores?

She was a chemically imbalanced, suicidal, self-destructive, neurotic, alcoholic drug addict. But I gently swept those micro–character flaws under a rug. I probably did it because her heart was made of pure, bona fide gold and her soul and spirit were free. They were so free, in fact, that at times they blew around recklessly.

Dolores could light up a room with her magic or weaken an explosive situation with a kind word. She always knew the right thing to say, the right thing to do. She was filled with song most days and walked around singing the only tune she had ever learned the words to ...

This little light of mine.
I'm gonna let it shine.
This little light of mine.
I'm going to let it shine ...

I used to hear Dolores sing that song in my sleep. She had so much charisma she should have been a movie star. Dorothy Dandridge didn't have a thing on Dolores, except a contract and some cash.

When Dolores entered a room the place lit up like an electric parade. She commanded the attention of everyone because she was the extraction of perfection. Beautiful like black onyx and raw like black coal. Illuminating like a black sky filled with brilliant stars. And mysterious like perishing meteors that evaporated before they could even hit the ground. But more than what she was or what she wasn't, she was special because she was Mama.

That's not to say that Dolores wasn't foul. She had some nasty habits.

9

Booze.

Drugs.

Men.

They all demanded something of her and one by one they took their toll. Over the years, I watched Dolores suffer and knew she was intimate with devastation, struggle, and crippling disappointment.

But it never changed how I looked at her. Sometimes she was high, other times she was drunk, but she was always Mama. My beautiful, black, Nubian, African queen.

We lived together for years, sharing everything from one toothbrush to a pee-stained cot with a hole in the middle.

The kitchen was a breeding center for roaches and members of the rodent family. At the breakfast table, it was best to cover your bread with your hand between bites. If you forgot, pieces of the ceiling would crash down and stab the bread to death.

In the bathroom you had to shower quick. The temperature outdoors used to hold steady at nineteen degrees and heated water belonged only to those who could afford their bill at the end of the month.

The cold, nasty water brought with it ice and sometimes sewage. The faucet had to be turned on with pliers because the handles broke years ago. In other words, it was no Taj Mahal, but it was home.

Sometimes I'd get a wild hair up my butt and complain about the accommodations.

I'd get sick of showering in filthy subzero water. My hands cracked and bled from the struggle to turn the water on and turn the water off.

I'd get tired of spitting out pieces of the ceiling that I accidentally bit into when I ate my toast.

I hated playing "dodge the defiant roaches" every time I needed something from the kitchen.

I hated sharing a toothbrush with Mama.

I hated getting stuck in the cot's giant hole and sometimes falling through to the floor.

However, that's not to say that there were no joys. There was joy.

I had been the proud owner of two pets I inherited from the landlord. They were fat rats with long, spiraling tails. One rat was an albino with pink eyes and the other black as tar with eyes dark as night.

I named the rats Honkee Honkee and Niggah Niggah. They'd curl up beside me at night, one at my head, the other at my feet. The rats were my friends. So naturally, you will understand my devastation when exterminators came out, sneaked into our apartment, went behind my back, and set up my playmates.

One night while sleeping I heard a metal rattrap snap and woke only to find Honkee Honkee twisted in the contraption, rolling violently through the kitchen cabinet, fighting death till he finally collapsed.

I pronounced him dead on the spot, gently closed his beady eyes and labeled it another ghetto tragedy: Honkee Honkee. Seven months old. Dead of a broken neck.

Shortly afterward, Niggah Niggah packed up and moved out. I never heard from him again after that night. But every time I saw a black rat on the street, I would stare into its dark eyes and call out in a hollow voice, "Niggah Niggah, is that you?"

But I never found him.

Losing Honkee Honkee and Niggah Niggah was a major loss in my life at that time. But little did I know that this was only the beginning of a life that would run rampant with loss.

As a kid growing up, I didn't mind living with Dolores. She was a lot of fun when she was sober. But the last time I saw her sober was when I was about three years old. After that, almost every night Dolores was incapacitated. She'd pass out naked on the cot with her tongue sticking out and legs gapped open. Sometimes she'd get so high she wouldn't wake up for days. Why do you think the cot had so many pee-stains?

Dolores came from a family of dirt-poor niggers straight off the plantation. She ran away from home when she was fourteen and moved to the land of golden opportunity, the Dorchester projects.

She worked a dozen jobs before landing something permanent. She slaved at a factory, a sewage treatment plant, a plumbing establishment, a lumber yard, a grocery store, beauty shop, and finally at an after-hours gambling joint. And it was at this gambling establishment that Dolores finally started making some money.

She'd been broke for so long that when she finally came up on some cash, she went buck-wild. She was obsessed by it all, the money, the men, and the drugs.

It was easy for Dolores to make money selling herself. She was fine and all of her parts were in the right place. Her hips curved, her butt was round, her breasts were pleasing to the eye, and her nipples stood at attention all the time. She had big brown eyes and a sparkling smile (at least that's what her pictures looked like).

To be honest, I don't remember the woman in the picture. When I was a little kid, Dolores was strung out on heroin. She smoked it. Shot it. Sniffed it. And would have swam in the shit if she could've fit her big ass into the little pouch of white powder.

Dolores was gentle by nature, but the drugs awakened a demon within. And when she lost the high, she was a woman gone mad and everything and everyone that stood between her and the next hit was going straight to hell.

I always knew when Dolores was going to lose it. She'd sweat so hard her clothes would wring with salty perspiration. After the wetness came convulsions. And sometimes her body's unannounced jerking "motions" put her at great risk of hurting herself. Once she almost bit off her tongue and another time she knocked herself out cold when she threw herself against a wall.

I would hide in the closet and watch Dolores through termite-eaten walls. And what I saw was never pretty, and more difficult to translate on paper. Her body slammed against walls without mercy or compassion. She would stand soaked in sweat and sometimes blood. Her hair would dance on end as her clothes hung from her frame. Her huge, sagging breasts would escape from her bra and take turns smacking her in the face.

Dolores had rolled around the room on the floor violently. I witnessed her body literally bend in two from the pain, which continued until she found the last vein in her arm to blow out with the needle. Every time she stabbed herself with the filthy needle, she prayed her vein had enough staying power, so as not to collapse in the middle of the rush.

Most days, her prayers went unanswered and the vein would blow out. I watched as Dolores literally beat her arm black and blue trying to find a vein that was strong enough to take the shot.

The scene was traumatic only until Dolores found the vein, and then, just like magic, the ghosts would stop their assault, the room would spin to calmness, Dolores would take a deep breath, and it would all stop. And then she'd start singing to the Lord right in the middle of shooting up, getting high.

This little light of mine.
I'm gonna let it shine.
This little light of mine.
I'm going to let it shine . . .

Maybe she felt closer to God flying on a high. Or it could be the drug put a little distance between her and the demons.

This drama played out every day in my house. And when it was all said and done, the place would be destroyed.

She would rip down curtains, break dishes, destroy bedsheets, and vomit without warning.

That was probably the biggest problem Dolores faced when she didn't get the drug on time: vomiting.

Upchucks for hours. One time Dolores threw up so long and hard she ruptured blood vessels in her eyes, leaving them blood-red for days.

I always kept a bucket by the bed because I never knew when to expect regurgitation. The only trick was to get Dolores to throw up inside the bucket instead of on the floor.

On the good days, it went in the bucket. On the mediocre days, it went on the floor. And on the bad days, it went on me.

As a child I did not find this repulsive. Nor did I find it unusual or disturbing. I was a kid. Dolores was my mother. Heroin was my stepfather. I just had a stepfather who mistreated my mother and made both of our lives a living hell.

CHAPTER TWO

Every hell comes with a fire escape. And when it got too hot I got the hell out. My escape came in the form of field trips with Dolores. Some kids went to the zoo, others to the park, but Dolores was unique in her parenting style. My first outing with Mama was to the whorehouse when I was seven years old.

Dolores called this raunchy place a "gentlemen's club." Yeah, right. The last thing you were gonna see in this stinkhole was a gentleman.

She'd lock me in a room in the back and whisper into my ear, "Stay here, sweet thang, while Mama takes care of business." She'd always leave me with a cup of apple cider, a coloring book, and an eight-pack of crayons.

I was never sure what was going on beyond the stained walls of my world, but when I was inside the room, I was always fascinated by the barbaric noises that echoed through the walls like an unrehearsed choir.

It went on for hours. Deep moans, squeaking beds, heavy panting, urgent and brisk dialogue.

At seven, I wasn't hip to the birds and the bees. I was still trying to break the code of the monkeys in the trees, so I just assumed the noises were folks expressing their appreciation for apple cider and coloring books. I thought it would be rude of me not to do the same.

So I began.

I would gulp some juice, then moan. I would take another couple swallows, then groan. When I finished the last drop in the cup, I would mimic the final climactic squeal I'd heard so many times before.

I continued this behavior until one night a big black cornbread-eating woman burst into the room and knocked the cow-waddling shit out of me. And from that day forward I never said another word.

It was as dangerous in my house as it was in the whorehouse. Dolores was hosting the show like a runaway train with bad brakes running on the wrong side of the track.

As a child I never understood how someone who was so beautiful on the outside could have so much wreckage on the inside. And just when I thought Dolores would overcome it, *could* overcome it, she backslid. Just when I was prepared to declare her "normal," she flipped the script and entered our home like a ghost I'd never seen before. She came in as a stranger, looking around our simple place like this was her first time here, picking up this, looking under that. Her paranoia was a constant, creeping around corners, peeping out windows. How could such a pretty woman be so battered and so blue? It was nobody's fault—

nobody's but her own, I guess. And that was hard for a kid to digest.

When Dolores passed out I would sing to her.

This little light of mine
I'm gonna let it shine.
Oh, this little light of mine.

It was the only time she ever listened to me, when she was under the sleep of unconsciousness. The other times I seemed not to matter much at all, though I tried not to take it personally. Not everyone can be an enthusiastic parent. Some people have children simply because their vaginas wear an OPEN sign. And that was life, or least life with Dolores.

I would brush her hair while she slept. It made me feel close to her, closer than usual. And I would have fantasy conversations with her. Well, it wasn't really fantasy because I was really talking, but the part where she was supposed to be answering back, now *that* part was fantasy.

How was your day, Mama?

Oh, your day was great, I said. *I'm glad, Mama. What? You got a raise? They gonna pay you how much money, Mama? Wow ... and they took you to lunch to celebrate? For real? You ate steak for lunch? What did it taste like, Mama? What, you saved me some? It's in the refrigerator? But, Mama, we don't have a refrigerator, remember? Oh, you bought one with your raise? Wow, thanks, Mama. I'm proud of you, Mama. I'm real proud of you.* But no sooner would I begin to believe the fantasy than it would be abruptly interrupted by Dolores's tremors, a calling card of the heroin. And I would retreat to a corner in search of safety as I watched and waited. I stood by helplessly as she suffered and more helplessly as I waited for the suffering to end. By morning it was over, with the only residue of the night before, a headache for Dolores, a heartache for me.

"Baby . . . coffee," she gurgled upon waking. She was so hung-over she could barely move. I poured Dolores hot coffee each morning. Every time I handed it to her, I wished the tiny grains were magic and that once she set the mug down she would be a different person than she'd been before she picked it up. Or at least a different person than she was the night before and the night before that. *This is your new day,* I always wanted to say. But more than I wanted to say it, I wanted to *believe* it. I had always hoped she would never find a reason good enough to do another drug or take another drink. But reasons that large would be difficult to materialize.

No one loved Dolores like I did.

No one.

And perhaps that was the most consistent reason why I always found myself excusing bad behavior, demanding very little accountability of her. There was a lot of pressure on Dolores, being a single parent *and* a heroin addict. It was best to be one or the other, but to be both, now, that was the definition of conflict. I reduced most of my mother's issues to economics. She needed money. And she needed it bad. In the end she may very well have been a drug addict and a dirty, nasty prostitute. She may have been as stupid as the day is long, but she was my mother. She was the woman who lent her womb so that I could flourish. This was the same woman who lay down and took the pain of labor so I could be born. Again and again, she was my *mother.* Everyone loves their mother without demanding that their love make sense.

I forgave Dolores for her absence in my life because that's what good kids did. It wasn't so abnormal, the disappearance of a parent. Almost everyone's parents were absent. Even the ones that bothered to come home at night still weren't really there.

Drunk on booze.

High on heroin.

Incoherent on crack.

Wearing married men's semen stains on their outfits like badges of merit for a hard night's work. Well, at least the rent would be paid, I guess. That was Dolores's story as well as her friends'. That's who they were. It wasn't open for judgment, analysis, or discussion. And we were their children, their seed, their product. Delivered to them on a technicality: *Oops, somebody got pregnant.*

I could see Dolores's insides and knew she was more than the war that she waged. Other people had opinions but their opinions didn't count because they didn't know her like I did. Bottom line, Dolores was a decent person with a good heart who was accidentally turned into a monster by the demons she got too close to. And that is my summation on the soul of a heroin addict.

CHAPTER THREE

Outside the doors of a drug addict and her illegitimate child, life was not trying to make up for its losses. My early days in the Dorchester projects were bleeding memories of times that should have been better than they were.

I candidly recalled such a time.

I awoke one night to a standoff between police and Dove Johnson. Dove was a twenty-six-year-old hustler who lived next door.

He had been hauled to jail a dozen times or more for petty crimes, but word on the street was Dove was dealing with foreigners. And the bigger word: Dove was making the money.

Even though I was only seven I wasn't so tender at all. I understood Dolores's drug lingo and was accustomed to the neighbors passing around each other's personal business like a secondhand crack pipe. I had a front-row seat in the arena of, *I know all your daddy's secrets 'cause your mama keeps running her big-ass mouth.*

I knew Dove was selling pure coke for rich Spanish-speaking folks down on the south side—south side of America, that is, not Dorchester. I'll spell it out for the slow ones: He was getting gigs from South America. It was estimated he was making somewhere between five and seven grand a week. And truth be told, Uncle Sam didn't dip 'n' dab in Dove's money. Dove didn't pay Sam shit.

I remember Dove standing on the street corner handing out hundred-dollar bills to the little nappy-headed, ashy-legged, latchkey kids after school. Dove even saved Dolores's butt a time or two with a rent payment here, a rent payment there.

Dove's life was an open arena of controversy. The older generation hated Dove for what he did. They said he dispensed drugs to the neighborhood and killed its spirit and people.

But the younger generation had a different view. They loved Dove because they saw him as a businessman who conducted his affairs as any ambassador would. Dove had universal appeal.

He appealed to the men because he was personable during his drug transactions. He made you feel like you were getting the best buy for your buck. And even though the shit he was selling could kill you, his sales pitch was so good he almost made you believe you were making a legitimate investment in your future.

Dove had magnetic appeal. He had dibs on every pair of drawers in the neighborhood because he had screwed everything in a skirt collecting a welfare check. At least that's what Dolores used to say.

Dove was a ladies' man but not much of a gentleman. He would be with Martha on Monday and Lucy on Tuesday. On

Wednesdays it was Carmen and on Saturdays it was Sandra.

It didn't hurt that Dove was drop-dead gorgeous, but it also didn't help much, either. Anything Dove couldn't buy, he could put on hold or loan by flashing those big white teeth and winking those flawless brown eyes with curly lashes. In other words, Dove was the cat's meow.

But Dove was more because Dove was smart. And he used the best part of his intellect to play a fierce game of cat and mouse with local police.

He was always under investigation, but authorities turned up nothing because Dove was a thinking man. And Dorchester police were not accustomed to dealing with thinking men.

But even the best player must rely on circumstance and good fortune. And the night I awoke to the Dorchester standoff, neither was in Dove's favor.

It was Tuesday night, so naturally he could be found at Lucy's. Word had it that Dove was knee-deep in Lucy's goodies. The place was rocking when the police interrupted the flow by making a broadcast over the loudspeaker demanding Dove's surrender. Since Dove was a thinking man, he automatically assumed the house had been surrounded and the chance for escape was minimal. According to Lucy, he had already begun calculating his best legal maneuver to avoid a trip to the state pen.

Dove was dropping knowledge on Lucy. He took her into the most sincere place of his heart as he divulged the secret hiding places of his money. Dove never used banks. He didn't believe in them.

Lucy listened intently to Dove's directions before throwing her arms around him in a desperate embrace. She was scared and needed to hold on, which was all good and fine, but in the meantime, police were getting restless.

Several minutes passed and still no sight of Dove. The cops didn't like it. People started jumping to conclusions, and in anticipation of violence they prepared for it.

The idiots in charge called for backup for the front line and backup for the backup. They called out sharpshooters, a SWAT team, and hostage negotiators. They barricaded the street and made the entire block their prisoner.

And there we stood at our front window, Dolores and me, watching it all. Absorbing the hate, the fear, the passion. The pulse of the street beat out of control, and in the final act all eyes would bend to the raging scene.

It was just like a movie, only better. There was no script. No direction. The final act was a bitter free-for-all where unpredictable characters acted more out of stupidity than instinct. But nothing could have prepared us for what happened next.

In the space of a moment Dove appeared from nowhere and ran across the front yard with a gun in each hand, shooting wildly at the cops.

The cops shot back, spraying the front yard with metal messengers, ripping through Dove's body, bringing a swift wind of death.

Dolores freaked out and started screaming. She closed the curtains and pulled me away from the window where I'd been held in a trance by it all.

"We gotta get out of this neighborhood," Dolores said. "I don't want you growing up with dead bodies all around you."

"It's okay Mama," I said, trying to reassure her that I wouldn't be scarred for life by witnessing an execution.

"No it ain't," she said shaking. "It ain't okay."

Dolores started pacing the floor, then sat on the bed and rocked back and forth without control.

"I'm sorry, Symone," she said. "I shoulda been a better

mama," she said, curling up into a little ball. "You ain't got no daddy. You ain't had no good home training. You ain't got no bed of your own. No room of your own. No toothbrush. Your shoes are raggedy. Hell, you ain't got shit..." she said, talking more to herself than me.

"I got you, Mama," I said, rubbing her head.

"And that's enough?" she asked.

"That's enough," I replied, sparing her the burden of truth.

I kneeled on the floor by her side and watched her drift into a sleep, then I returned to the window where I watched the coroner zip Dove into a plastic bag and carry him away.

Nervous cops, dark nights, black men with firearms, junkies working overtime, single parents, crazy kids, dying people, dead people, and toothbrushless homes with broken dreams—it's simply not *enough*.

CHAPTER FOUR

I found very little need to confirm the existence of a ghost. There was no urgency to create a father so that I could be someone's daughter. It just didn't matter that much. But I did learn details along the way because eventually everyone must know where they came from.

According to Dolores my biological father was as white as the Easter Bunny. And in my 'hood, Dr. King's dream of equality was still a long way from realization. Black and white only went together on hot fudge sundaes and piano keyboards. Dolores never wanted people to know my father was white, but the blue tint to my eyes and the blond streak to my hair just gave the shit away.

Blacks thought I was a confused white girl who wanted to be black. Whites called me "niggah lover." At a young age I learned society would never give me the luxury of being both, so I had to decide which side I would play on.

I decided to be black.

My neighbors were black. My peers were black. My mentors were black. Even my shoes were black. But that's not why I chose to be black. I chose to be black because Dolores was a Negro. And if Dolores was good enough to be called a Negro, then so was I, though I often found myself questioning that decision.

"What am I?" I often asked Dolores, but only when she was sober, so that I stood a chance of a decent reply.

"What are you?" she repeated, cockeyed, confused. And I would take it upon myself to bend her attention toward the color of my eyes and the texture of my hair, making a case in point to note that we were *different*.

"Mama, what am I?"

And her answer was always the same: "You are a rare and beautiful bird," she said while cupping her hands around my cheeks. And I would feel special. I knew Dolores loved me because when her eyes were not under the influence of demons and heroin I saw love inside of them. She loved me as best she could, but it never seemed enough.

There were days I felt particularly void of a spirit and a soul. And on those days I pushed for answers to ease the burden of the loaded question, *Who am I?*

"Oh, I remember," I would begin each discussion. "I'm a bird . . . the rare kind, right? Well, tell me about the father bird," I would ask my Dolores. Not that I gave a damn about him, just thought it would make more interesting conversation than she and I could come up with on our own.

Dolores said she hooked up with my father one night while pulling a double at the grocery store where she worked as a clerk. Supposedly, this Caucasian gentleman came through her line sporting a double-breasted suit. His scent and charisma stepped before him and Dolores was sucked in by the energy that pulled her to him. She couldn't claim it or name it but knew she had to have it.

"What's a fine thing like you doing in a dump like this?" she asked, reeling him in with her smile. According to Dolores, he held up a package of gum and replied, "Pit stop." Dolores was always attracted to a man who was clean and a man who was rich. And from the sounds of it, this man was clean *and* filthy rich. And Dolores, well, she always had a way with the fellows, white and black alike. She seeped sexuality, erotica oozing from her pretty black skin. All she had to do was wink those big eyes and part those full, pulsating lips smeared in red lipstick, and usually—not all the time, but usually—the man was hooked. And this man was no exception.

Dolores winked as she teasingly handed him changed for the hundred-dollar bill he had just deposited into her hand. He winked back as if to say, *Keep the change.*

When he walked out of the store, Dolores literally walked off her job and followed him to his hotel. She strutted boldly to the front desk, where she befriended the hotel's desk clerk. And soon thereafter the clerk gave Dolores the white man's room number.

Dolores hightailed her coal-black ass up to his door and knocked. One thing I can say about Dolores, Dolores had a whole lot of nerve.

The white man answered the door, looked at Dolores, and invited her in. The short version:

They did it.

Dolores missed her period.

Nine months later, I'm here.

Next?

The pregnancy wasn't planned and no one was expecting me.

I didn't come home to a decorated nursery and a whole bunch of fools singing, *Goo-goo, gaa-gaa.*

I was born at a local hospital in the back room of an unsanitary maternity ward.

The mortality rate for newborns at the dump was two-to-one. I beat the odds that day. I lived.

The on-call doctors were bottom-of-the-barrel. They were young, inexperienced, and overworked. They were incompetents who got off on the title "doctor". They came with big egos, bad attitudes, and degrees from poor universities. They didn't give a damn about the sixteen-year-old unwed teenager who had just given birth to the three-pound premature baby with underdeveloped lungs. How could they? Two doors down, another baby had just died and the mother lay on a table bleeding out. And in between deliveries they were faxing job resumés to anybody that could transfer them to a name-brand hospital and deliver them from the hell they simply referred to as "County General."

The next day Dolores was released from the hospital. She caught the bus home and we set up shop in a studio apartment in a nearly condemned building with our new neighbors: rats, roaches, and convicted felons.

Dolores said she never spoke to or saw my biological father again. She never told him she was pregnant so he never knew about me.

So there you have it, the unedited version of my white daddy as told by my black mother while high on heroin.

Dolores refused to tell me his name because she feared that someday I might go look for him. But little did she know I never would have gone looking for him. I was too busy looking for myself.

My childhood was sketched in inconsistencies and confusion. I was round and the rest of the world was square. I looked white on the outside, but felt black on the inside. I identified with the struggles of my black peers, but could never be a part of the struggle because they treated me like I was white. I was a minority who looked like the majority. I was odd man out, but in a white man's world I could blend in. And so why was I complaining? Because my Caucasian look didn't give me insight into the Caucasian world; therefore I remained a resident, but was always treated like a stranger in my own neighborhood.

In addition to my racial identity, or lack of one, I noticed an attraction toward people of the same sex. As early as age seven, I was drawn to little boys *and* little girls, unjustifiably aroused by them both. And I never wanted to contemplate the horror of being a little of both, a girl *and* a boy inside. No one had told me *no*, to my thoughts on "acting out" with both sexes, but creatures are born with an internal monitor pushing them away from the like sex. And this is how procreation continues. If we didn't, we would mate with our own kind and eventually die off from Earth. My childhood issues of sexual confusion led me in search of a map so I could sit down, pull out a pen, scan the continent, and find myself.

Perhaps it goes without saying that I never fit into anyone's world. How could I? I was a bisexual, biracial, blonde-haired, blue-eyed niggah white girl from Dorchester. I was unscripted and jagged around the edges. I was awkward growing up and even more awkward grown. My existence ran the course of zig-zagged lines. My life would never bend in the direction of straight. It would always take a turn, maybe a twist. And fate would see to that.

It began at the age of eight. I had elements to contend with that came with no understanding. I could *see* things, visions. They weren't creepy things or eerie things, just ugly things. I witnessed the goings-on of other people as though I were standing either in their rooms or in their bodies. I was privy to the cryptic details of tormented lives without the courtesy of gossip.

My neighbor, thirteen-year-old Loretta Jones, didn't tell a soul that the child she carried belonged to an uncle. But I knew because I had seen with my own eyes how her uncle had taken advantage. And it was their secret and my secret till Loretta cracked up and the whole ugly truth swam out.

I also knew Dolores was trading her body for money. I saw it in my sleep, an intrusive vision that left me in my sweat and then in my tears. I called these visions "night sweats" because of the sour smell of raw perspiration which enveloped me upon my waking. It was sweat so violent it could have melted my skin off had it not been calmed by the mist of damp air. For those reasons, and more reasons, I was lonely as a child, lest somebody call me out and say I was a *freak*. I spent many years as a loner, disconnected from the cruelty that being "different" brings. I stayed inside my skin and kept quietly to myself. My arms didn't reach too far, and neither did my heart. And then one day, to my surprise, I unzipped and came outside.

CHAPTER FIVE

Ina Boone was my best friend.

I was seven. She was nine.

We were both in the same grade. I was advanced one grade because the teachers thought I was brilliant. Ina was held back a grade because the teachers thought she was slow.

So this is where we met. Somewhere in the middle, caught between our slow but brilliant lives.

I was on the teeter-totter, waiting patiently for the next putz to come, sit down, and try to outride me. I had a bad rep on the totter, known for riding cruel, hard, and fast. On several occasions I had even thrown a playmate or two off the board, sending them flying into the air with their only cushion being the crust in their unwashed underwear.

I was the teeter champion. And no one with half a wit would

go up against me. So imagine my amazement when Ina, a scrawny, ashy, bucktoothed, four-eyed girl, came and sat down on the other end of the teeter-totter.

I was more dumbfounded than impressed. I had more pity for her than compassion. Could this skinny little heifer be challenging me? Didn't she know who I was?

Without warning, she threw her body back, and *up* she went. *Down* I went.

I pushed off the ground with my strong, vibrant legs and up I went.

Down she went.

I let out a monster groan and *up* she went.

The skinny little diva let out a growl and I was *up*. And so went the battle, filled with a sea of unpleasant sounds and body language.

Our production was drawing a crowd. The kids on the playground were stupefied by the competition. This scrawny little wench and I had turned the playground into a war zone.

When the mandatory first-hour warning bell rang, no one budged. When the second bell squealed *ding-dong*, still no one moved. The second bell was serious.

If you missed first-period roll call you were marked absent and your parents were called at their jobs (those parents who had jobs).

The teacher would chew out your parents and challenge their child-rearing technique.

If this happened, it was best to run away from home, because when you got there you were greeted with a list of *(a)* new rules, *(b)* new chores, and *(c)* an ass-kicking that started in Cleveland and ended somewhere in Puerto Rico.

But everybody on the playground that day was willing to risk it. They all stayed through second bell.

When Miss Hogie, the school's warden/principal, set her big size-eleven shoe down on the playground's dirt, we pretty much figured the ass-kicking would be sooner rather than later.

Hogie, wearing a bright red two-piece polyester suit that accentuated her fat ass and dragging boobs, was headed our way.

Her relaxed hair was holding on to very little of the homemade perm she had put in just days prior. Her flesh was jiggling and I could tell by the magenta tint to her hairy face that she was a tinge disturbed.

But by this time the crowd was already in a frenzy. It was time to call in the riot police because the nappy-headed little kids on the playground were going hog-wild.

We all knew it was just a matter of moments before Hogie would rain on our parade.

I looked at scrawny Ina and she looked at me. We both knew it was now or never. But before I had time to do a damn thing about it, Ina pulled a fancy, illegal maneuver, which sent me flying through the air.

I remember looking at the faces of all the kids, and wondering why all of their mouths were open. Probably because I was flying through the air like a bird without wings.

When I woke up, Dolores was standing over me in the nurse's office. Principal Hogie and scrawny Ina were also at my side. The nurse was eagerly monitoring the lump on the back of my head.

"The nurse thinks you got a concussion," Dolores said.

"Cool," I said, closing my eyes because there was less pain if I didn't have to look outside of my head.

On that day I got my first concussion, lost my first competition, and found my new best friend.

Over the next several months Ina and I became inseparable. We were like twins, connected by bone, blood, and mass. By the end of the school year, I had fallen deeply in love with her.

The kids used to look at Ina and say her ugly ripped from the tip of her head to the floorboards beneath her feet. But I saw a beauty that was scorched to the bone. I refused to think of her as anything less than beautiful.

Sometimes we would deceive the night and stay up till morning. On one such night Ina looked at me and offered the most beautiful bucktoothed smile I'd ever seen.

"What is you?" she asked quietly.

"What?" I responded.

"What is you?" she repeated.

"I am a rare and beautiful bird," I replied confidently, but she wasn't buying it.

"Your mama's black but you don't look black," she persisted.

"But I am black, Ina Boone. I'm black as you."

"But you don't look like me," she said, brushing her rough hand against my soft cheek.

"But I am like you," I offered in my defense.

"What kind of bird did you say you was?" she asked.

"Rare and beautiful," I repeated, but Ina just rolled her eyes. "Maybe you just black on the inside," she said, resting her cheek against mine.

After that night, I spent the rest of my summer vacation in the sun trying to get black like Ina. I teased my hair and tried to convert my naturally wavy texture to a kinky, tight curl pattern, but it didn't work. My hair turned against me and matted on the ends. Dolores ripped through it with a comb, tearing most of my hair out with it. And as for the sun, it only turned me a bright shade of red and burned the mess out of my skin. I gave up. It was too hard being black.

Ina lived about two blocks from me, but she may as well have paid Dolores rent because she was always at our house. We ate

36

together, slept together, and bathed together. At seven years old, I knew I had found my soul mate.

Ina was still teeter champ and we were bitter rivals on the playground. But when the game was over, we went back to loving each other again.

Ina and I used to walk the grounds of the school hand in hand. I didn't think it odd, and just assumed that was the way you behaved when you loved someone.

The older kids snickered and called us gay. I didn't know what gay was, but I knew what love was, and if loving Ina was gay, then I guess gay was an okay thing to be.

And on those nights when Ina's mother wouldn't let her stay at my house, I would stick my head out the window before I would go to bed and shout down the block, "I love you Ina Boone! I love you!"

And some nights I could barely hear a whisper in the wind sing a gentle song: "I love you back. I love you back."

Ina was an artist, the very first one I knew.

She had a gift for restoring junk. She would take a primitive thing and re-form it. Ina's jewelry was nothing but pop-bottle tops. Her clothes were recycled rags. Ina's hair ornaments were tossed aluminum twisted into ponytail holders. She had a reverent appreciation for art. At least that's what she called it, art. But most people would never see what Ina saw.

I remembered one afternoon on our way home from school she came across a butterfly that was dying. She picked up the butterfly and held it in her hand till it died. Of course, I thought this was peculiar behavior. Ina took that butterfly home and the next time I saw her, she had made a necklace, which she had strung through two pieces of glass pressed together. And inside of the glass there lay the intrinsic wings of the butterfly. It was so simple yet so beautiful. So unimaginable from the onset that I dared to call it bizarre. Who would think to create such an ornament? She tied the necklace around my neck and this became our friendship token. Every time I looked at the necklace I longed for Ina's gift, the ability to envision what others couldn't see and the sense of know-how to force it to be. Yes, that was Ina's gift.

She spent the summer teaching me her passion, explaining, instructing, and guiding my eye.

One day, while walking through a desolate park that boasted broken, rusted swings, dead grass, and flesh-eating mosquitoes, Ina stopped.

"What?" I asked, thinking she had lost something.

"What do you see?" she asked me as her eyes searched the emptiness.

"Nothing," I said, looking around.

"There's got to be *something*. Look again."

"Okay," I replied, this time looking harder.

"I see a broken swing. Bugs. A nappy-headed little boy looking for his mama. Ugly trees, dead grass, and a whole lot of weeds 'cause this ghetto park don't have a lawn man."

Ina laughed.

"What?" I asked.

"Is that what you see?" she asked, poking her finger into my head. "Is that all you see up there?"

"Yeah, that's what I see."

Ina shook her head.

"What do *you* see?" I posed the question to her. I surely had to know.

Ina stopped laughing and started speaking. Her tone was flowing and mellow. "I see sad trees that look like they need a hug.

Sad grass crying for some water. Broke swings that need some-body to play with. I see life . . . I guess. That's what I see, Miss Lucy."

Ina always called me "Miss Lucy" when she was trying to make a point.

I looked out at the old, dead park again.

"You see what could be and not what really is," I said.

"Yes," she said with conviction and a naughty little grin.

"But I do that every day, Ina . . . every time I look at my mama."

I didn't respond but she understood. I, too, had my own form of vision. The balance of the afternoon we sat under the sun absorbing the warmth of its heat.

Ina was a dark and lovely animal. And me, I thought of myself as a caramel-colored creature. We held hands, sometimes ex-changing looks.

Ina was serene. Solemn, but peaceful. I was enamored of her beauty and mesmerized by her flawless black skin, which lay across her body like a dark satin drape.

When I first laid eyes on Ina, I longed to tame her proud African features. I wanted to dim her blackness and exchange her African heritage for a more Caucasian look. Slim down the nose, heighten the cheeks, soften the bubble in the lips, and relax the curl of the hair.

Originally I failed to see her beauty. But that day, with the sun tipping gently against her, beauty was an unconquerable force, which ruptured through the holes of her soul.

"God, you are beautiful," I said.

Ina kissed my cheek softly and stroked the ends of my hair ever so lightly. I closed my eyes and soaked in the sun and the warmth of her touch.

Was this gay?

It felt good when she brushed against me. She tickled pleasure zones.

"Are we gay like the kids at school say?" I had to know.

Ina paused a long time before responding with a definitive, "I don't know."

"Do you want to be gay?" I asked.

"Do you?"

"Don't see why not," I said.

"Okay."

Ina and I spent the rest of the day roaming through the neighborhood telling the neighbors we were gay.

By the time I got home, Dolores was waiting in the front yard with a stick. I spent the rest of that hot summer night in my mother's living room getting my ass beat.

Being gay.

Big mistake.

Life in the big city kept spinning. Dolores was pulling doubles back-to-back at the club. She was still getting high to cope with reality and I was still anticipating the arrival of her new day. I never saw much of her anymore, but there were sightings here and there.

Like one day, Ina and I were shopping downtown. I really shouldn't say "shopping" because neither one of us had a dime. Actually we were looking and wishing. Translation: Looking for shit we wished we could buy.

We took a fancy to a particular kiosk in the center of the courtyard. The cart's display of exotic earrings, necklaces, and bracelets invoked the greedy in me. Oh, how we longed for *anything* on that cart. So imagine my reaction when the gatekeeper of the jewels bent down and offered Ina and me two of the most beautiful jade bracelets I'd ever seen.

My mouth dropped from ceiling to floor. This was surely a

mistake. If I accepted the bracelets, the gatekeeper would summon the police and they would storm in and arrest us for shop-
lifting. I stole a quick glance at Ina; she was looking more like
a criminal by the minute.

"No," I said to the fat lady.

"Go on. Take them," she said in a tame Jamaican accent.

"We have no money," said Ina.

"None," I reiterated.

"They've already been paid for," she said.

Well, I had a hard time believing that considering the hanging
tag still said, bold as day, *$60.00.*

But then I looked around the corner and I caught Dolores
winking at me. She was hanging on the arm of a white man who
looked to be heavy with cash.

I smiled back and mouthed the words, *Thank you.*

Dolores briefly looked back two more times over her shoulder
as she disappeared into the dirty afternoon air. I knew she was
well into her heavy drug-using days, but even under the influence of all that is unholy and despicable, trading her body for a
puff of the white powder, she was still the most beautiful woman
I'd ever seen.

That was the last time I ever saw Dolores alive.

CHAPTER SIX

It was the saddest day of my life.

June 17 and shortly before my ninth birthday, I awoke to find
Dolores rigid and lifeless, her body unyielding to breath, movement, or the vibe of living. I thought she was sleeping, or should
I say, hungover from the night before, but when I brushed my
hand against her skin her body was an eerie cold. It wasn't the
kind of cold that you and I experience. It was the kind of cold
that was an indication that all systems were down. I put my ear
to her mouth and listened for shallow breathing but there was
nothing but silence screaming back.

My dear, sweet, drug-addicted, alcoholic mother; my first, my
last, my Nubian queen, my everything, my world, my laughter,
my joy, my pain, my longest day and darkest night, my greatest
hope and Mama, *dead.*

Again. Dead.

Her eyes were open, her once-sultry lips, cracked and split down the middle. Dolores was gone. Finally gone. Really gone. She had been to the edge a thousand times or better, but this time she wasn't coming back.

A one-way trip, final deposit.

No return.

Entrance only.

No exit.

I also knew that where she was going, I could not follow. The chill on her flesh exemplified the great distance now between us. She belonged to the dead, and I, for the most part, was still among the living.

I wanted to cry.

And fall apart.

To writhe, scream, and suffocate myself in a wiry blanket of pain.

This hallucination was my life.

This nightmare was my dream fully awake.

I wanted to hold on instead of falling or come together instead of splitting apart in a thousand unreachable, unfixable, un-mendable pieces. It hurt so bad at the time that even blood flowing through my veins seemed a horrible inconvenience, a painful and debilitating bother.

Grief.

The painful, gut-wrenching ache that twists and contorts without mercy. *Oh, have mercy. And let me die, and break, and tear in two.*

But I couldn't. If I broke, I wouldn't come back.

Not ever.

I kept my composure and remained unusually calm. For in many ways I was intimate with the lifestyle of the stoic.

At the age of eight, death was like my next-door neighbor. I saw it every day. I had stepped over the brain matter of a guy whose head had just been blown off during the dispute of an unpaid loan in the amount of $2.73 plus interest. I had played dodgeball next to decaying corpses that nobody bothered to call in till after the game was done. Blood and guts didn't upset the balance of my daily routine because it *was* my daily routine.

I sat down and poured myself a bowl of corn flakes. I drowned the flakes in government milk and tears. I'd finally let them go, the tears, making a swift exit from the Stoic's parade. The tears came with violent force, hot and sticky, reminding me that I was mortal; I was reminded through Dolores's death and my life and every single beat in between. I could not see where the spoon ended and the corn flakes began because so many tears were in the way.

After I finished my cereal, I put on some clothes and went to a pay phone to call Ina. After Ina, I dialed 911. I told the operator Dolores was gone, really gone. She said they'd be right out. They showed up two days later.

Bastards.

Ina came right over and allowed me to collapse into her tiny little arms that for the moment seemed so strong, so big and essential for keeping me whole and in one piece.

We sat in the apartment for two days and watched Dolores turn colors and her body swell to twice its size. She began to decompose right before our eyes. After the first day the smell became so putrid, Ina and I both threw up.

Ina begged me to come to her house but I couldn't leave Dolores alone. Dolores and I promised years ago that we'd be together till the end.

"But this is the end!" pleaded Ina. "Come on, Miss Lucy, let's go."

"Ina," I said looking dead into her black eyes, "I am not leaving this house till Dolores is picked up and safely on her way."

Ina knew there would be no argument. The blind allegiance of a child to its parent knows no compromise.

She shuffled back inside the house and sat down next to me. My mind was made up and so was hers. Both of us would see this through to the end.

It was spooky spending the night with a dead person, but when Dolores's decomposing body started to move, that pretty much sent me over the top.

Insanity. Dolores would sit straight up, then fall back down. A leg would jerk, an arm would twitch and her mouth would fly open. Her body expelled gases. In other words, Dolores was farting. Have you ever heard a dead woman fart?

A couple of times I thought she'd cheated death and come back to life, but the undertaker said it was just air and raw nerves.

The coroner ruled that Dolores died from an accidental overdose. It may have been an overdose, but it was no accident. Dolores was tired of living as a slave to the substances she abused. Sometimes, when she was in her right mind, I believe she, too, remembered the woman she used to be.

In my heart, I know Dolores was a good, honest, decent, loving, and lovable human being who just didn't do well with the hand she was dealt.

No big surprise to find out that, after Dolores died, she didn't have a lick of insurance, so the state threw her in a box and tossed her in a cemetery with the balance of life's impoverished and dejected members of society.

The only three people who attended her service were me, Ina, and Ina's mama.

The funeral was short and sweet. The preacher said Dolores

was born and Dolores died. He concluded the service by saying if God was feeling merciful when Dolores passed, she "might" be in heaven. Otherwise, she was burning in hell.

Amen.

Amen.

Amen.

At the cemetery I stared at Dolores's casket as the final prayer was offered. And I couldn't help but shift my eyes to the other graves around me, most of them unmarked. It seemed so cruel to live a lifetime, only to wind up one day in a pine box with a handful of people to come and say good-bye. And of that handful, the majority would be so unaffected they wouldn't even shed a tear.

"Life is for the living," I had heard Dolores say once before. "Put the dead in the ground and then get on with it."

And that's just what everyone did. They got on with it. Ina's mother kissed me on the cheek and Ina held my hand for the last time.

"Where will you go now?" asked Ina.

"To that place . . . ," I said, staring hard at Dolores's closed coffin.

"What place?" asked Ina.

"The place where things can be . . . ," I said.

And then Ina smiled.

And, surprisingly, so did I.

And we both watched in silence as the casket sank into the ground. After Dolores was laid to rest I stood by her grave for quite a long while before whispering, "Mama, this is your new day."

After the funeral was over, the state of Massachusetts sent a car to pick me up.

As for Ina and me, it was a simple good-bye. I could not bear the weight of a dramatic exit.

"Miss Lucy?" said Ina.

"Yes?" I said, from beneath tears.

"You're my best friend," she said.

"And you're mine."

"And that's enough, right?" she asked.

"That's enough," I assured her.

"I wish you could come with me," she said, "but Mama's not well," she said referring to her mother's crack and prostitution habits.

"I know," I said softly. Everybody had a habit in our neighborhood. It was the only way people knew how to survive the reality of it all. I had never done drugs and neither had Ina, but inadvertently we understood their place in our world. And we both respected it enough not to try and change it. Not that any of us delighted in watching our mothers self-destruct but we were too insignificant to intervene. How could an eight-year-old speak louder than crack?

I offered Ina a single kiss on the cheek. Opened the car door. Stepped inside. Shut the door. I looked straight ahead most of the way, but at the end of the road, I turned around for one last look at the skinny little ashy legs. Buckteeth. Twisted glasses and tornado hairdo. And that was the last time I ever saw Ina Boone. Three years later she would catch a bullet in the brain during a drive-by shooting.

CHAPTER SEVEN

I was declared an official ward of the state. I was an offspring of the government and they screwed me sixty-nine ways to Sunday before it was all said and done.

I was an eight-year-old, broke, illiterate, black orphan with blonde hair and blue eyes, daughter of a druggie who had just died of an overdose, and who in the hell was going to bring me home for keeps?

When Dolores died, the ground opened up and the world swallowed me whole without chewing. I belonged to the people, but they didn't want me. No one wanted me . . . till the Hustons came along.

On August 17, eight weeks after Dolores died, Ridge and Madeline Huston, like two Caucasian miracles, walked in through the front door of the orphanage, took one look at me, and said the magic words: "We'll take her."

I packed up my belongings and kissed the ghetto good-bye. I was still illiterate. Still black with blonde hair. Still sexually confused. Still sad about Dolores. But now I was about to be something I had never been before: in the company of a lot of money. And even as a youngster, I understood what it means to be part of the world of those who have and those who have not. I was ripe for a change because impoverishment never did suit my style.

We drove for hours in a fine Mercedes. I had never been in a car with air-conditioning. On hot days in Dolores's raggedy car, the only way to cool down was to spit on yourself.

I sat in the backseat trembling, fearful to move. The environment was sterile, uninviting. The Hustons were like wax figures. Their posture impeccable. Their image, untouchable. I had never been exposed to people like this.

Their speech was soft, and gestures polite. I was accustomed to shouting and loud talking. I found myself constantly straining to hear what was being said. I wasn't sure if it was because I was partially deaf or they were somewhat mute.

I felt painfully intimidated, fearful that someone would address me and I would be forced to respond. My language didn't flow like theirs did. My words weren't exotic and my accent wasn't pleasing to the ear. I probably talked too loudly, too jagged. And more than likely my nouns and verbs were at war with one another.

Ridge Huston would turn around every now and then and wink. This made me extremely uncomfortable. The only time I had ever seen people winking was when they were seizing from a drug overdose.

I couldn't get over these rich, white angels. I stared and

gawked. I was behaving so poorly, these white folks probably thought Dolores forgot to teach me manners. But I did have manners. I just couldn't help myself. I was simply mesmerized, especially by Madeline.

She was elegant, smooth. Her hair was whipped into place, wrapped in a sweeping bun held together by a most unusual hairpiece. Madeline's clothes were exquisite, her accessories impeccable. Her jewelry was obviously the best money could buy. Her stance was wealthy and unshakable. She seemed like the unsinkable *Titanic* (and we all know how *that* story ended). From the tip of her coiffed head to the bottom of her manicured toes, her appearance screamed, *I am the birth child of cold, hard cash!*

To my amazement, even the powdered makeup which covered her pale complexion was wealthy.

I knew the makeup was rich because it was a hundred and two degrees and it didn't melt off and dribble down her white cheeks like it should have.

In my neighborhood on hot days like this, poor sistahs went au naturel. In other words, naturally, that cheap-ass, swap-meet makeup would melt off when the temperature rose above sixty-eight.

Everything on Madeline was enchanting. And in my ghetto opinion, she looked like a queen.

I sat in the backseat taking in her odor. Her exquisite scent reminded me of fresh tulips growing wild. Not that I'd ever smelled a wild tulip. The only things growing wild in my neighborhood were weeds and untrimmed afros.

But Madeline's perfection didn't end there. I appraised her head to toe and made a firm assessment. Her dress was perfectly pressed and noticeably crisp. It bore no creases, wrinkles, or mustard stains.

She wore a stunning pair of summer sandals that commanded your eyes. They definitely weren't like the crap Dolores used to buy from Ziggy's One-Stop Shoe Drop.

After my studies, I concluded Madeline could definitely be classified as "fine." But her beauty was much different than Dolores's. Dolores was fine in that she was beautiful without the glamour and Madeline was beautiful in spite of it.

She spoke painfully proper, and offered plastic smiles between long pauses. Her aqua eyes were piercing, her skin shamefully fair, and her blond hair glistened. And yet something about Madeline didn't work, didn't fit, wasn't genuine.

Key pieces of the puzzle vanished midair. Looking at her was like staring at a circle somebody forgot to close. You knew the lines were supposed to meet, but for whatever the reason, they didn't. I couldn't be sure things with her were really *wrong*, but something just wasn't *right*.

Now, Ridge Huston, he was impeccable. *Impeccable* was a word I'd learned from Stivey Down, a local drug dealer and mentor to the kids in the neighborhood. I thought the word was appropriately applied in this situation. Ridge looked too clean, like his soap and water cost more than the average person could pay for such amenities. His skin looked like a baby's butt, and later I would learn that this was partly due to the gentlemen's facials he received on a weekly basis.

Ridge was a handsome man, and there was no denying him that. His features looked like they had been set to music. He was wearing a black suit when they picked me up, the kind I only saw at funerals. And around his neck there hung a purple-and-black tie. I had never seen a purple tie before. And his shirt was purple, too. Maybe purple was his favorite color, and had I not been so intimated by his larger-than-life presence, I would have asked. *Excuse me, Mr. White Rich Man, but is purple your favorite*

*color? And I'd also like to know if collecting orphaned Negroes is
your hobby* . . .

But I wouldn't dare ask him such questions. He didn't look
like he played at all, and it probably would take next to nothing
for him to snatch off his belt and take to whooping my ass.

I didn't know his story but I knew he was important. At the
orphanage, the caseworkers had made a big *to-do* over Huston.
They catered to him and fed his ego. They eagerly followed him
around like they were waiting for a gold coin to pop out of his
ass, but it never did. And even if it had, I doubt he would have
shared it with them. He didn't appear to be the sharing type.
But what did I care? The only lucid thought I had as the Mercedes pulled up to the wrought-iron gate of this massive estate
was: *Why did these white people drive to a black neighborhood to
find a black girl who looked white to bring her home and raise her
as their own?*

Oh, why?

CHAPTER EIGHT

It was the biggest monstrosity I had ever seen and they called this beast their home. It was hulklike in nature, and intimidatingly huge. *How did you get so big?*

I slithered from the backseat and was swallowed by the shade because the sun got lost behind the concrete.

Madeline Huston put one arm around me and whisked me away while Ridge remained behind, attending to the details.

We were greeted by the gardener, who smiled at Madeline and cut me with his glare as if we had met before. He offered the bitter expression when Madeline looked away. *Sneaky little man,* I wanted to say as we crossed his path.

"Come . . . come," said Madeline, rushing me, pulling me. "I want you to meet your sisters."

The strain on my face dictated I had no interest in meeting

anyone new and even less interest in calling them "sisters." But there was no room to step outside the box and complain. I had been advised by the orphanage to be a good little girl lest I find myself returned. And if that were to happen, my return would not be pleasant. "So don't piss them off," was the last of their words, "because if you do, you'll be sorry."

Thoughts of the past were flushing me out and so were my thoughts of the present. Where had I come from and where was I going? Who were these people and why did they want me?

"Come, come," Madeline rushed again. "There's no time to sightsee," she scolded as I paused for the beauty of it all, trying to absorb the interior majesty of the house.

"Save it for later," snapped the lady of this house. I was beginning to ponder on changing her name from Madeline to "Miss Pushy."

"Do you ever get lost in here?" I asked, making notes of the exits just in case.

She laughed out loud, "You're such a witty girl!" she exclaimed. "The orphanage really should have told us how witty you were," she said sarcastically, making me feel like a charity project. *Adopt a Negro on Tuesday and earn extra points toward that dream vacation.*

I wasn't trying to be witty. Wit wasn't my objective. I simply wanted to know how they moved about this giant maze without being eaten by it.

"What do I call you?" I asked her.

"What?" she asked, taken aback.

"You and Mr. Huston, what do I call you?"

"I never thought about it," she replied blankly.

"Do I call you 'Mama'?" I asked.

"Oh, no," she responded abruptly. "You must never call me 'Mother.'"

"Why?" I asked.

She stopped walking, put one finger on her cheek and waited till the lightbulb went on inside her head, "Because . . ." She paused. "I'm not your mother," she said. "Call me Madeline."

"Okay," I said, not giving a shit. I didn't want to call her "Mama" anyway so she did us both a favor. And the only reason I asked in the first place was to save myself the trouble of pissing them off.

It was awe-inspiring, this place they housed their bodies. I had never seen beauty like this. I had never even dreamed beauty like this. My imagination wasn't large enough to fit a house this size inside. I didn't belong in a world *this* pretty. And as long as I never forgot that point, it would save me the embarrassment of trying to fit in.

We arrived in a room they called the "main den."

I was brought back to reality by the biting voice of a child snob. "Her name is *what*?" asked the little angry girl referred to as Audrey.

"Symone," said Madeline, "this is Audrey, my eldest child."

Audrey was fair, ghostly-white with curly black hair, and dark, dark eyes. She looked like an expensive porcelain doll wearing ruffles, lace, and hard, shiny shoes. Perhaps she had been kept on a shelf her entire life, barely allowed out of her box to play. She looked hateful but maybe she was just bitter to have been crowned princess without consenting to the role.

"Audrey, say hello to Symone," prompted Madeline.

Audrey stared at me a long time before responding, "Hello." It was dark and echoing, the way she said "*hello*." It was obvious the little bitch didn't want me in her house.

"And Chandler," said Madeline. "Come out from hiding." She

walked around the room like a nut talking to herself. "Come out from hiding. Come out from hiding."

And soon this pudgy girl resembling a little piggy stepped onto the floor and gave the shyest smile. She was also fair, with chubby cheeks and a red nose. She wasn't dressed delicately like Audrey; instead she wore overalls with a denim hat, hiding her plump body. I doubted this was the child that made Madeline proud. No, this was probably the one concealed behind excuses, fat farms, and polite non-observance. This was the one to be paid off with food and hidden treats. Madeline would probably give Fatso a whole box of Twinkies just to keep her off her nerves. Audrey was the representative and Chandler was just the child. But I liked the little blimp. She was the only one who appeared normal, whatever "normal" was.

My meeting with the girls was brief before I was whisked away again. Madeline dragged me down a hall and deposited me in front of a door.

"This is your bedroom," she announced. And when she opened the bedroom door I swore I was dreaming.

There was a giant bed in the center of the floor with four big posts soaring toward the sky. It was grandiose. Majestic. The bed was made of material I couldn't even pronounce and the Hustons had had it flown all the way from Italy just for me.

I couldn't believe I wouldn't be sharing this bed, not even with the ghost of Dolores. Would there be no one to battle for a soft spot in the middle? No legs to throw aside in the middle of the night? No arm to put back in its place? No urine to clean up when accidents happened?

The room was decorated in a deep, rich, emerald color with bloodred highlights. The room was so exquisite that even the doors had their own nationality. I believe she called them French.

The bedroom had its own private commode. Madeline referred to it as "the powder room," but there was no powder in the room. There was a toilet, a sink, and a fancy bathtub.

A tub with no leaks, a commode that flushed, *and* a working faucet was almost too much to ask for in one lifetime.

Was I being greedy?

I was afraid I was going to wake up to find a cruel joke had been played on me. That I was going to lie down in this fancy Italian bed tonight and wake up tomorrow morning in the Dorchester projects.

I stood in the center of the room, afraid to touch anything. It was all so very beautiful. I was secretly waiting for the real owner to come in and toss me out onto the street in the middle of the night. I would exit through the French doors and wander aimlessly around until I found my way back to my real home in the ghetto.

Later that night as I sat in my new surroundings feeling like Alice in Wonderland, I was quickly snapped back to reality by the thunderous voice of Ridge Huston as he shouted from the long hallway outside my door.

"Chandler! Chandler! Where are you hiding?" he howled.

Heavy steps echoed through the hall, moving closer toward my door.

"Chandler!" he shouted, "Daddy's looking for you." He came and stood right outside my door.

"Have you seen Chandler?" he asked me.

I could have easily said no. In truth, I hadn't seen Chandler in some time. But just as he uttered her name I saw her face.

There she was, standing in my room, hiding in the dark, seemingly propped against her shadow for protection. I had not seen her enter, but how could I have missed her? Perhaps she'd slipped inside when I'd stepped into the potty. And were it not for the fear on her face, I might have blown her cover. I was about to point, blow a horn, and hang up a sign announcing Pudgy's presence.

But I didn't.

Her eyes alone told a story.

"No," I lied, without flinching an eye. "Haven't seen her."

"No?"

"No," I said.

Huston stole a peek into my eyes, and I into his. He knew I was lying, but it didn't matter because he couldn't prove it. And I could bluff the devil out of hell if I had to, so I wasn't worried I'd break.

"You sure you haven't seen her?" he asked.

"Yes."

Huston reached into his pocket, pulled out a hundred-dollar bill and waived it enticingly through the air before reinserting it into his pants.

"No?" he asked.

"No," I said. My eyes were unchanged, my stance unyielding. Did Huston believe I was so desperate he could buy me? Did he think that just because I was poor I had no worth? I'd seen Dolores sell herself a thousand times over for cash and it had never made her rich. So what was selling out Chandler, a scared little six-year-old, going to get me?

"No," I said again, but this time with attitude.

He backed off and closed my door. As my eyes peeled to the corner I saw Chandler shaking like a boneless puppet. And where she stood, there was a puddle.

The scared little blimp had peed on herself.

It was then I knew there was more to this story than could ever be written on the page.

CHAPTER NINE

Night sweats.

Night sweats were my dance, especially in the Huston home. They were a continuation of the visions I had experienced in Dorchester, only here, they were much more violent. This was my first indication that something here was very, very wrong. But I could not call it out yet. This evil did not have a face nor did it have a form. But it had a life and I felt that pressure on my spine.

Each night I would bathe till the flesh nearly fell off. Afterwards, I would saturate myself in oil and lotions. And my feet, the two little distinctive devices attached to my ankle, they were my passion. I loved my feet and always gave them special attention.

I would court each toe one by one: oil, massage, and tend to them. I would stroke my greasy hands against the heel of my foot, especially the ball at the base of the heel.

Ritualistically I would pour powder over my entire body, drowning my frame in the absorbent cornstarch, which would cling to my body from the moisture of the oils. And then I would lie down.

But without fail I would wake to night sweats. It was my plague. I would rise from a sound sleep nearly dead by drowning in the pool of my perspiration. It would drip aggressively down and around my throat. Without permission it would slide down the front of my chest and roll over onto my back. It was prohibitive, incarcerating. In the wetness I felt caged.

And with the night sweats came the nightmares, images I experienced somewhere between sleep and waking.

I was at war with my wetness: lie down dry, wake up drenched. And in the end I was powerless to find the water's source.

Disturbing.

The distorted images disengaged me from reality. I felt suspended, disconnected, and sometimes insane in the morning when I would awake.

I saw the future looking through a hole in the past, tragically linked to the present. And this was unexplainable. Unimaginable. *What was this I saw?* A world not so pretty, and perhaps this was the earliest indication that my life would soon decline.

I had a sense that things around me were false. I had an urge to call them out and claim they were an illusion. I felt uneasy breezes blowing between my toes.

In my sleep I experienced images so horrible I was forced to keep one hand on the sun at all times, lest I slip and lose sight of the light.

And this is where darkness and I lost courtship.

Darkness went from a natural progression of losing light, to an iron cage and a solid, gelled structure leaving me no room to breathe.

Powerless.

In the dark, the demon moved without supervision. He matched his strength against mine and I lost every time.

Violent acts.

Vile acts.

Crimes against humanity no one wanted to discuss over morning tea.

And when I awoke I wasn't sure if I had dreamed a nightmare or lived through one in the dark.

Dolores had believed I was a prophetess. She was convinced that my night sweats were visions of things destined to be. Dolores said I had "the gift." She believed I could see vile creatures who had taken on the form of man. Dolores believed. I didn't. But I should have.

About a month after my arrival, one night while caught between sleep and wakefulness, annoyance crept into my soul. I heard an odd sound, like light, echoing thunder. I tried to ignore it as I tossed, turned, and tossed again.

I stuffed a big white fluffy pillow over my face. This was not an attempt to suffocate myself entirely, but just enough to calm the "pattering" sound against the walls.

Once it became apparent that I could not quash the distraction, I sat straight up in my bed. This much I do remember. And from where I sat, I could see the little snob squatting on the floor, bouncing marbles off my wall. She threw one marble after the other. There was no rhyme, reason, or motive, just an onslaught of marbles bouncing off the walls.

As I studied her disturbing behavior, ironically, she studied me back. Her eyes hungered for knowledge of who I was and where I'd been, as she pierced me completely, through and through, with cold hard stares.

"What?" I called to her. "What are you doing?"

She did not answer.

"Why are you bouncing marbles off my wall?" I asked.

No answer. And that's all I remember. When I woke in the morning there was no one there.

No Audrey.

No anger.

And there were no signs of a disturbance against my wall.

There was just me. And I was consumed by the sweat of the night as I sat in my bed, drenched in my own secretions.

"Why didn't she answer me?" I questioned aloud. "Why was she throwing marbles against my wall?" Suddenly, it all began to sound so absurd.

"Of course she couldn't answer me," I said aloud, again. "She was never really here." And with that, I resolved the drama of the night by concluding it was just part of another episode of night sweats.

As I pulled myself out of bed and shuffled to the bathroom to drip myself dry, something rolled beneath my feet, nearly causing me to fall. I couldn't believe it, but there it lay beside my foot, a single, sparkling marble.

The next night was worse.

I felt trapped by two dancing shadows in the far corner of my bedroom. There were two intertwined bodies holding on to one another passionately.

"Deeper," a woman moaned. "I said *deeper*," panted the familiar voice.

"I'm in as deep as I can go!" a man's voice responded.

"I can't feel anything," said the woman.

"I don't know what to do," said the man, growing more agitated.

"Make it longer," said the woman.

"I can't," said the man.

"Bigger?" said the woman.

"Can't," said the man.

"Then harder!" the woman demanded.

"I can't," the man said weakly.

"Why?" cried the woman.

"I've already come," admitted the man.

The woman shoved him and their bodies unglued.

I thought my eyes had gone mad, for I could not believe what I saw: Ridge and Madeline Huston, standing in a pool of body secretions.

Through a crisp silhouette I could see Madeline's nakedness. I saw the curves of her hips and the firmness of her upright breasts, with erect nipples.

I could also see Ridge's nakedness. His large frame bore a limp and crooked penis. It looked as though his penis had been sewn by an arthritic seamstress. From the distance it looked weathered and worn, tattered and used. It was an essential part of his manhood, this I was sure of. I just couldn't figure out why it looked so ready to fall off.

"You just can't get it right, can you?" said Madeline.

"What do you mean?" he said, lowering his head.

"Why do I bother?" she snapped.

He said nothing.

"I just want to come! That's all I want, Ridge. I want a big, huge, gushing orgasm!"

He lowered his head, defeated.

"You were *always* weak," she said, pushing past him.

The prim and proper Madeline slid into the night, dragging her flesh and perversions behind her. And with her exit, gone, too, was my respect for the woman I thought I knew.

The circle had just closed on Madeline, and to that end I etched her appraisal in stone: a sexual deviant. One who creeps through the night heightening sexual pleasure by performing erotic acts in the presence of children.

When the room was empty of all but me, I sat erect in my bed, unable to peg my feelings. Perhaps it was fear, perhaps excitement. Had I really been privy to such a private act? Or again, was I simply dreaming?

I was frightened of the changes within my own, pre-woman body. And though my mind found Huston's act despicable, as I watched I could not control the swelling of my own vagina as it doubled in size and began to ache. I had brushed against erotic feelings before, but this time it felt much different.

What was I to do with this surge? . . . arousal? . . . And the rush I felt beneath me?

If I closed my legs tight and squeezed them together would it go away?

I tried it. I closed my legs. I squeezed. But that only made the sensation stronger.

I squeezed again yet it still grew stronger.

I squeezed once more only to find it ever-heightening.

What if I sent down my hand to part the lips and force them to attention?

I did.

"Oooohhhh," I said aloud.

A big, huge, gushing orgasm.

I lay back a moment and took it all in, reflecting on the drama playing out before me. Originally I had summed up the world of the Hustons as sterile, rigid, and protected. I didn't think the

Hustons were much like real people. I was afraid their "sterility" would rub off on me and that they would teach me to become them, to *be* them. I was horrified that if I learned too many of their ways I would lose my own. And eventually, piece by piece, limb by limb, I would disappear, leaving behind very little evidence that I was here at all.

There were so many inconsistencies around me. So many elements rooted away from truth. And although it had only been a month, "pretty" was peeling away. I couldn't see what was beneath the surface but I was certain it was rotten.

Ridge and Madeline were pigs, no doubt. And perhaps I should have been disgusted. But I concluded you'd have to do more than the nasty against a wall to shock a girl from the Dorchester projects. Madeline's unique bedside manner, surprisingly, affirmed one simple fact for me: she was almost human.

And what about Ridge Huston—what was his real story? He was powerful and influential, no doubt, but in all that boasting, he was still a man unable to satisfy his wife's most basic needs, though, really, there was nothing basic about Madeline's needs at all.

This did not banish my horror; it simply added new dimensions to this nightmare. But that was only the beginning.

Over the next several weeks they were back, night after night, positioning themselves awkwardly in my world.

She continued to dominate. He continued to be weak. And in between thrusts they would argue incessantly. She demanded he get it up. He would come to his defense by insisting, "It's up!"

And me, I simply continued to sweat.

No more was I caught in the world of uncertain reality. This was real, all right. And with that, my night sweats took to the day, where all I did was sweat.

Sweat. Sweat. Sweat.

I tried to bear up under the weight of reality. But reality never did anything for me. It only took me a little deeper into myself where I struggled to climb out of the catastrophic wishing-well that I had fallen into while hanging too far over the edge in search of a wish.

I could have been traumatized by the two freaks who consumed one another against the walls of my room. But I chose instead to disappear. I realized disappearance was a viable option, especially since truths were starting to spill out onto the floor and folks were slipping and sliding in them by accident. The lie was the truth and the truth was the lie. And that's what I learned early on.

I also learned that the White House was black and the black house was blue and the blue house had been burned to the ground. Mister Rogers never visited my neighborhood and Big Bird was pushing crack at the other end of Sesame Street. Elmo was masochistic and Oscar the Grouch was an undercover pedophile who used his trash lids to cover naughtiness. And this was how I passed my time, amusing myself with wild ramblings in exploration of uncut imagination.

I loved to make up stories, creating them from nowhere and exaggerating truth. At the age of ten I began writing a story that would take years before its completion. It was a fantastic voyage that took my breath, soul, and body away from the present and put me somewhere else.

It delivered me to a tiny village too small to name—a unique town of deaf-mutes where no one uttered a sound. This city of mutants was governed by the only speaking person in the village, Abigail. She was my hero, standing six feet six inches tall with bronze skin and long black hair that ran all the way down past her knees. Abigail had one giant brow in the center of her forehead because both brows arched on end and met themselves in the middle. She represented physical perfection and her interior and exterior were both unscathed. She was just and fair, strong and mighty, passionate and dominant, loyal and full of integrity. Her heart was made of precious metal, constructed of gold and crucified against her chest cavity in black iron. She was indestructible from the inside out, the deaf-mutes' messiah. Abigail was everything I wanted to be. I made sure of that because I wrote her that way.

She was the mother I never had and the father who didn't exist. She was my best friend, Abigail. I dreamt about her when I was sleep and talked about her when I was awake, but only during conversations with myself. I never shared Abigail with the world because the world was unworthy of her. And I never would have wanted the world to become dependent and rely on her as I had come to do to get me through days and nights, and nights and nights. If they came to depend on her then perhaps I would lose her to them. And I couldn't afford to sustain the great loss.

I trusted Abigail.

I trusted her more than real people to do the right thing because I controlled the pen and the pen controlled the moves. And no one made a move until I said they could. And the moves were always right because I was the writer and I saw to it.

As the days grew long and the nights even longer I relied on Abigail more and more. She was no longer simply the deaf-mutes' messiah. She had also become my salvation. She would save me again and again, and every time I picked up my pen to write her story, my own journey bled through and the village would be rescued and, also, so would I.

PART TWO

CHAPTER TEN

I hadn't been to Eden in about a year and the only reason I was coming today was to make an appearance, which in turn would purchase me another year of absence. I came to the estate once every ten to twelve months, for obligatory roll call. But today was complicated because Huston had called a family meeting, which was quite atypical of the norm.

I had driven up that morning from the city with my boyfriend, Teek. The closer we got to Eden, the more agitated I became.

We checked into a modest inn because God knows I had no intention of spending the night with those motherfuckers on top of the hill.

After check-in, our first stop was a local café. Once inside, I took in heavy stares from local busybodies. I caught meddling housewives staring at Teek, probably eye candy for those horny bitches, and the prettiest thing they'd seen in years.

Teek was tall and olive, built and booming, the son of a Portuguese mama and Italian daddy. He had a fresh face with sharp features and was easy on the eyes.

They wanted to know who we were, the locals.

They wanted to know if we were gay or straight, lovers or friends. They wanted to know if we had money and if we belonged in these parts.

They wanted to know if we were nomads who had simply happened upon their elegant town by mistake, happenstance.

Suburbia wanted to know.

The flowing conversations prior to our arrival tapered off to chopped sentences with bridges, gaps, and pauses once we had entered the room.

I wanted to throw up. I didn't want to be here. It was obvious we weren't welcome. Once we were seated even Teek caught the vibe.

"Are you comfortable?" he asked.

"No," I quickly responded.

"Then maybe we should go somewhere else to eat—" he suggested.

"There is no place else," I injected sharply, cutting him off.

"There aren't any other restaurants in Eden?" he asked.

"Of course there are," I snapped. "But they're all the same."

"They don't like blacks around these parts, do they?" he asked.

"You have to ask?" I posed the question, which gave way to the answer.

The rest of the breakfast was uneventful, the food bland, and the atmosphere never evened out to a comfortable blend. Surprise. Surprise.

We ate.

I paid.

We left.

And from the moment we ascended through the winding roads toward the Huston estate, I could literally feel myself starting to change.

I punched in the four-digit code on the security entry panel at the gate and it opened like a womb delivering a child. I still got pains in my stomach watching the steel expand, appearing as if it wanted to embrace me for a moment before coming in for the kill when I turned my back. But that never happened because I *never* turned my back.

I found myself aroused as I watched the gate open because I knew if I chose to stand in the center of its clutches, it could've crushed me upon closing. Perhaps it was the thrill of being so close to death that I found erotic. But I pushed that aside knowing there would be no orgasms today.

And every time I pulled my goddamn car through those gates I asked myself the same questions: *Why are you here?* And, *Haven't you had enough yet?*

I was usually lulled into a false state of security by the beautiful scenic drive through the winding mountains. The majestic countryside that surrounded the estate was like a shot of novocaine, it numbed me just enough so I wouldn't flinch when the Hustons went for blood.

They were family but I struggled with the concept because for the most part I despised them. I often likened them to an abscess, an open sore in desperate need of closing.

I never was a Huston, at the core. The Hustons were chameleons in disguise, ostentatiously displaying a pretense of the pious.

I have morals. Respect me. Respect me. The fact that I'm sleeping with your spouse does not make me immoral. For I have purchased an honorary membership into a society of the moral and righteous. I am so wealthy that should I be tainted by bad conduct, I have enough collateral to ensure the return to purity.

And this was their lament.

I must be a fool. Why come back? Was I coming to even the score or to finally make things right? Or better yet, was I returning to rewrite a past that had already been etched in stone and sealed in blood?

I should have had my head examined for stepping foot on these grounds again. And I should have been locked up for bringing an outsider in.

But what the hell? It was Thanksgiving Day and I could afford the struggle with my inner demons to share a single meal with these godforsaken people I called my next of kin.

I searched my purse for a Valium as I pulled my red Explorer through the mighty gates. Every time I entered the grounds I dropped off into the same fantasy. I'd dream of blazing through the fortress armed with a flamethrower that I'd discharge without hesitation, blowing the whole compound to bits and pieces.

I didn't fantasize about such violence because I was innately drawn to it to fill in the empty space between my quiet thoughts and the louder ones. That wasn't my pull, but justice was. *Eye for an eye, remember? Tip the scales and make them even.*

If you only saw the drawbridge before the manicured flowerbed that stood over a man-made lake in front of the Roman columns of the house, which dropped behind the sunrise that looked like it was painted by God, perhaps it *was* beautiful. But if you saw what I saw . . .

Teek was riding in the passenger's side and when he took in the panoramic view of the estate, his mouth slipped to the floor.

"Shit!" was all I heard him say. "This is your folks' house? This is some impressive shit . . ."

I wanted to bark at him for being in awe. If he had grown up here he would know that there was nothing on these grounds worth oohing and aahing over. But I couldn't fault him because he didn't know. I didn't have the heart to go the distance and deliver answers to him without proper explanation. And that's what it would take to enlighten him: proper explanation.

I just couldn't do it. Emotionally I tilted toward bankruptcy, struggling to balance between pain and healing. Up until a week ago, I had had two lovers, the pretty boy by my side and a fawn named Natalie. Yes, my other lover was a woman. She was timid and majestically concealed from the rest of the world. Natalie was easily startled. She made slow entrances, rapid exits. However, I beg you not to be so quick to call me out as gay. I wasn't gay, just not entirely straight. Or not so straight that I could bear to pass them by—vaginas, that is. They were a necessity, an awakening. And my passion for them fit together like the rest of my life: vertically, asymmetrically, horizontally, upside down, right side up, back side down, behind the front of the back. That was my life, remember? Twisted.

For the greater part of my life I regarded myself as asexual. I identified my sexuality from a neutral position. Life was just easier that way. It was almost simple to disregard my sexuality because sex had always translated to pain. And yet in fact I did enjoy my first lesbian encounter one hot summer night with Ina Boone when she placed her hands between my legs and did a wild rubbing motion. I found that I liked it though we never went farther than that.

I went many years without arousal after Ina, and in my late teens when I began to explore my sexuality again, it was with men, not boys but men. Not women but men. There was something fascinating and alluring about male anatomy and perhaps I was more curious than aroused but I can't be sure. I wasn't sure of anything except that I didn't do it on purpose, ending up with a boy *and* a girl. And I tell you this as honestly as a girl walking a straight line on a crooked path can say, but, strangely, it had played out that way.

Teek, Natalie, and me. From the outside world it would have been easy to judge us. And that's why we seldom shared ourselves with the outside.

We had a cozy arrangement. And then one day, and without warning, it collapsed like Enron stock.

Shattering me.

Shattering me hard.

Natalie left for no particular reason other than the one we give when a more noble excuse is unavailable: "We need to take a break," was all she said on the day she moved out.

"I didn't know that we were *breaking*," I replied, devastated upon learning the news.

"Yes," she said, gathering her things, refusing to make eye contact, heart contact.

"Why are you doing this?" I asked her, crushed under the weight of it all.

"Because I just can't do this anymore," she said.

"Is it me?" I asked.

"No, it's *me*," she answered.

And that was the very worst kind of answer because it offered no insight, just left empty holes for me to fill. Who was I to hold her down? And if I truly loved her, there were only two options: either set her free or hunt her down and kill her. Therefore I chose to set her free, though it cut me to the core.

Before our relationship deteriorated, I thought I would keep it forever—not the people, just the situation. Teek gave me things only a man could provide, whereas Natalie gave me things I needed from a woman. It was the order of nature: Monday through Wednesday I devoted my attention to Teek. He lived with me full-time, however, Thursday through Saturday, I was Natalie's. And Sundays belonged to me. Natalie kept her own apartment across town but spent about three nights a week with me. Natalie and Teek were special because they weren't consumed by one another's presence in my world. Teek spent a lot of time pumping iron, which afforded Natalie and me time for "girl stuff." The foundation of our relationship was respect. Teek and Natalie respected their space and stayed out of mine. They weren't evasive and didn't threaten me, because they didn't want all of me. Perhaps it was selfish on my part to dictate such a regimen, but I couldn't do it any other way.

There were no other men in my life and with good reason, Teek was *all* man. He was so smooth his walk was a glide. His voice so mesmerizing, that even if he cursed you out, you'd shake his hand and thank him for the conversation.

He dripped sex appeal, from the way his lips were pressed against his face, to the piercing depth of his hazel-colored eyes, down to the birthmark on his baby toe. The man turned me on. He was combustible like a nuclear explosion.

The sex was ripe, tight. We feasted on each other often, scouting forbidden places to baptize one another in wetness. Any place that was bold enough to try and contain us became our destination.

Once we made love in the broom closet of a crowded gym, and another time, the backseat of my Explorer in the middle of a busy parking lot during rush hour. We did it on a school playground in front of the principal's office. Several times we climbed on top of stacked pine boxes in an abandoned warehouse behind my loft. We did it on private streets and public streets. As lovers we were animal-like, acting on instinct as we made love to one other from morning till night. The sun set with him on top of me and rose with me on top of him. We devoured one another like cannibals. Our days together were bliss and then there were days, plenty of days, when I could not stand to touch him.

Teek was passionate about his workouts and his body was his claim to fame, with a sculpted chain of hard, linked muscle. Naked, he was the most beautiful creature I had ever seen. He was a well put-together package on the exterior, but every relationship must bear the burden of internal hiccups.

Teek spent numerous days unemployed. He was a laborer by trade but he labored very little because work was unsteady. He had never gotten around to joining the union so it was difficult for him to get a stable gig. This translated into meager finances, which meant that some days I felt more like a sugar mama than a girlfriend.

I loved my beautiful brown man but his finances were so weak that even Happy Meals were a hardship. But when my pretty boy did have money in his pocket, he treated me like a queen. It was just the in-between times that were tough on us: in between his last paycheck and the next one coming.

You do have another check coming, right, baby? I would ask. And his reply—a terminally predictable, *Eventually.*

Well, hell, *eventually* couldn't pay shit. Sometimes I even contemplated cutting Teek off; not because I thought he was using me, but I was disappointed because he wasn't using *himself*, his talents and gifts to make enough shekels and come correct with the rent.

Boo, I'm a little short this month, opened the first day of every month we saw together.

Again?

Next month is going to be better, I promise. But if you can just cover me . . .

Covered, I always said, coming to the rescue. And that was the end of it. At least till the next month and then we'd reconvene, same time, same predictable station. My tolerance for his lack of ambition (read between the lines: *laziness*) was endless. *Next month* never came, *next month* never did.

No relationship is perfect, and many aren't even close. In fact, most are brilliant examples of intricate dysfunction carried over from our childhood like birthmarks. I stayed with Teek because I loved him, not boasting that our love was a perfect love, but at least it was real.

We were entangled, he and I, and would remain so until one of us found a way to exist without the other.

Now, as for Natalie, she was a different type of bird, or "deer," as I affectionately called her. My thoughts on her are nothing more than obsessive reflections of a past that should have been released a long time ago.

Natalie was much more refined than Teek but eccentricity danced around her. She was half-and-half, attracted to both men and women. But she had only entertained me in *that* fashion.

Natalie was beautiful, erotic, and constant. She served as fascination for me because I had rarely seen anything so beautiful be real. She downplayed her breathtaking looks by living in faded jeans, dingy white shirts, and simple, unpretentious skin. She didn't like heels and pantyhose. It wasn't her style.

Natalie had been all over the world, a student of international travel. She had an insatiable appetite for lovemaking, and allergies to heavy commitment. She worked as a print model. Those of extraordinary beauty can always find ways to make "pretty" pay their way through life. And Natalie was so gifted at it. I had often wished Teek could have learned her way. Her easy, eloquent, unrestricted, free-flowing way.

Natalie chanted in the morning, meditated at night, and practiced yoga in 105-degree rooms. She was always "sneaking" away to attend secret meetings.

"Where were you, Natalie?" I would ask.

"Away"—her only and every reply.

"Away where?" I prodded as curiosity pricked me.

"Away-away," she would say. It was like a nursery rhyme and Natalie was like a child, concealing little red books behind her back.

"What are you hiding behind your back?" I would ask.

"The same thing you're hiding in your heart," she'd reply.

You win, Natalie. You win.

I loved Natalie because she was sensitive and gentle. It was easy for her to bypass complication. She was the girl who always stepped over the dog shit and I was the girl was always stepped in it. She was a gift that happened into my life by accident and I loved her for everything she was, wasn't, and wanted to be. But mostly I loved her because she wasn't *me.*

Natalie was ignorant to the pain of my past because I could not bear to burden her with my wounds. Therefore, out of respect for her place in this world as "drama-free," I never brought it up. Any of it.

I miss her, can't you tell? I'm pining away for a ghost.

"I can't believe this place!" said Teek, still rambling on.

I rammed the car into park without responding. Tension took over and I sat there like a ghoul in a cemetery. Teek looked at me anxiously, like a child preparing to enter a theme park.

"Are we getting out?" he asked.

I nervously lit a cigarette but did not respond.

"What's the deal, baby?" he asked again, pressing me, denting me. "Are we getting out?"

"Back off, Teek," I snapped. He didn't say another word, just stared at me.

I took a drink of soda water and swallowed pretty hard. I smoked my last cigarette past the butt and waited. Suddenly I was very angry and seething in bitterness. But it was wrong to direct such emotion toward Teek. He didn't know. He simply didn't know.

While we sat parked on the other side of the drawbridge, the gates opened again and a Mercedes blew recklessly through the opening.

The driver was a flamboyant blonde. Her hair was flowing, skin glowing, and practically every inch of her 44Ds was showing, except the nipples. She was outfitted in leather.

Boots.

Pants.

Vest.

Hat.

Purse. And her hands—well, let's just say diamonds were this girl's best friend.

She was a showstopper.

Teek was blown away, I could tell, but her beauty didn't phase me. I'd seen it all of my life and was privy to the fact that this girl's beautiful body and face were courtesy of some of the world's most talented plastic surgeons.

Her ass had been a Christmas gift and some poor bastard donated $6,000 to the "I need a bigger, better chest" fund four years ago. This girl had an aversion to the word *work* and a permanent hard-on for being a homewrecker. She was a twenty-six-year-old snob who had never got over herself as a child.

She was well groomed, had more raw materials on her body than the earth's natural crust. How did I know such things? Because this was my sister Audrey and I knew her very well.

Audrey disapproved of my lifestyle. She ridiculed my bisexuality and often referred to me as a freak. Not that I gave a shit because it wasn't like she was up for any Morality of the Year awards. Name-calling was done behind my back but tall walls inside massive estates have giant ears. *I heard you, Audrey. I heard that.*

Our sibling rivalry began years ago and it happened on Sunday morning; not just any Sunday morning, but a very special Sunday morning. For this was the morning that Madeline would parade Audrey and Chandler before a prominent agent of an elite New England modeling agency.

I wanted no part of this event and declined Madeline's invitation to participate.

Madeline spent weeks in preparation. And when all was said and done, a $25,000 *Woman's Day* brunch was catered in honor of the girls. She decorated them in elegant dresses and exquisite jewelry and hired a team of professional makeup artists and hair stylists.

An elite guest list was created and filled by the town's most wealthy and influential. And as they arrived one by one, I watched them from a tiny window tucked away at the back of my bedroom. And from the window I had a clear shot to those who entered and exited our home.

I peered into the souls of the glamorous women who waltzed their way to the entrance. They drove up in fancy cars with shiny wheels and catchy plates.

I had good sense, and good sense had told me a long time ago, *We may be in a different ride but we're all on the same road. And in the end we shall all be poured out at the same destination.*

And that's when she saw me, an elegant, dark-skinned woman who exited a long black Mercedes.

Timeless.

Stunning.

Mysterious.

I was impressed. Not because of her beauty. Or wealth. Or style. Or depth. I was impressed because she was the only one who looked up.

As the afternoon drew to a close, I found myself lurking around the kitchen in search of a decent plate of leftovers. As I tried to make a subtle exit through the common walk area I bumped into the agent Madeline had invited from the modeling agency.

When our eyes met, her face broke into a smile. Before I knew what had hit me, she grabbed my hand and marched directly to my stepmother.

"I want *her*," she said with strong confirmation.

"What?" asked Madeline, nearly spilling the contents of her mouth onto her lavish gown. Audrey and Chandler drained off all noticeable color.

"What's your name, dear?" she asked me.

"Symone," I said.

"But . . . but . . ." sputtered Madeline, "Chandler and Audrey are the models, not Symone."

"On the contrary," said the agent. "She's simply stunning."

Stunning?

No, not in a big white cotton shirt and tight little jeans. Not with hair hanging against my face without direction. Not with my lips smeared with the Vaseline disguised as lip gloss. No makeup. No bra. No shoes.

I was me.

Needless to say, Madeline was irritated and everyone else . . . flabbergasted. Especially when I turned to this talent agent, who as far as I was concerned had spent too much time bragging on me, and whispered politely into her ear, "No, thank you."

Her bottom jaw dropped.

The afternoon ended with the agent disappointed, Madeline

disgusted, and the girls discouraged. And as for me ... well, I was just happy there was enough food left to fix a decent plate of leftovers.

Audrey disliked me from that day forward, not that she was ever intensely fond of me prior to that day. She claimed I had raped their bloodline and used it like a leech.

But in *my* dictionary, when I looked up the word *leech*, there was a picture of a pre-surgery Audrey with a flat chest, a fat nose, and no butt that could be visibly captured on camera.

By the time Teek and I finally got out of the car, Audrey had made her exit from the Mercedes and bounced in our direction.

Her six-inch heels dug trenches in the cobblestones as she jiggled toward us, swinging everything that wasn't glued down. Her perfume was so strong it arrived long before she did and her weave was so stiff it looked like it was wearing *her*. Her fake nails were long and ravishing, painted with the bloodiest of reds, and her makeup was caked on so thick it could've put Duncan Hines to shame.

"Smooches," she crooned from a distance.

I was polite. I half smiled.

She extended her arms for a hug, but I stood frozen, unable to extend mine. Teek, being the jokester he was, reached out to embrace her. This unexpected gesture took Audrey aback a bit. Having a sense of humor never had been high on her list of priorities.

Teek burst into laughter and Audrey and I just stood there like retards. I couldn't remember a more awkward moment. Actually I could remember, but why dredge up such horror on a sunny day?

"And you would be ... ?" Audrey asked as she pulled her sunglasses down to check him out.

"Teek," he said, extending his hand for a shake. Audrey could barely bring herself to shake his hand and though he was beautiful, she appeared terrified to touch him.

"Don't worry, Audrey, I made sure he had his rabies shot before I extended the invite."

Audrey shot a look my way but nothing was said. After a long painful pause I made a bad decision to go inside.

I forced myself to put one foot in front of the other as I descended down the cobblestone path to the house. The journey was a weary one and my legs trembled uncontrollably. I had a death grip on Teek's hand. He didn't say anything, but I got a sense from the deep expression on his face that he knew. And for a moment I was so ashamed.

I slowly closed the door behind me and confronted the demons that came to greet me, the *memories*.

The inside was still beautiful and so lavishly decorated that it distracted from the *ugly* I'd known here as a child. The rugs from Persia, the marble from Italy, and the furniture from the Chinese Dynasty. But it was the sculpture of the naked man with the erect penis that took me back again to Madeline's *Women's Day* brunch. It took me back to the elegant woman, the one who'd exited the long black Mercedes.

The day she left the brunch, I'd stood at the top of the stairs, mesmerized by her beauty from a distance. Her body was long, narrow, and flowing. From both ends of her existence, feet to head, her gifts were evenly distributed. Her arms were slender and legs sculpted. Her hair was majestically black, stealing most of the attention from her beautiful face. Tiny spiraling curls draped against her eyes for decoration and they danced against all she turned her attention toward. Her scent was breathtaking as the smell of high-dollar perfume leapt from her skin without reservation.

I stood there barely breathing. Soaking her up like a biscuit absorbs the gravy. She escorted herself to the door but just before stepping outside, she stopped, looked around, and slowly approached the naked statue.

She took the large penis into her hands and gently stroked it up and down, down and up. Back and forth she went with such precise movement that it made me wet down there. I couldn't believe this elegant, illustrious woman was masturbating one of Madeline's favorite art pieces.

I was taken by the moment until this mysterious woman raised her eyes toward Ridge Huston, who was standing at the opposite end of the room, also caught up in her rapture. My heart skipped, then paused in nervous anticipation of what would happen next.

The woman made an exit that was dramatic and sudden. Ridge also retreated to wherever it was that had called him out. But I was still here, an audience member with nothing left to view, swelling with infatuation of this strange woman. And even in her absence it felt very much like she was still in the room.

I decided to follow her allure as I traveled down the steps and out the door to the black Mercedes that was parked outside. Cautiously I approached. The windows were tinted and the car appeared to be abandoned and looked rather lonely, boasting of beautiful blackness that begged to be caressed. So I did. I extended my longest finger and gently rubbed the car from hood to hubcap.

The window suddenly dropped.

"Don't touch the car," she snapped.

I stopped.

Would she scold me? Would she charge me for the car wash? Or worse, would she force me to wash her entire car to teach me a lesson?

"What's your story?" she asked.

I balked. "What?"

"Your story. What is it?" she said again.

"I don't have one," I replied defensively.

"Everybody has a story," she responded.

"Not me."

"Are you sure?" she asked with one brow raised.

I nodded.

"Get in," she insisted as her face gave way to a smile. I didn't respond so she repeated, "Get in. I don't bite."

With great hesitancy I opened the door and slid into the passenger's side but I didn't say anything. And neither did she, for a beat. Slowly she reached into her purse and pulled out a cigarette, which she offered to me.

"Don't smoke," I said, with a little bit of attitude.

"No?" she asked with interest.

"No," I repeated flatly.

"You look like a smoker," she said.

"And you look like a lady so I guess we're both wrong."

"Oooh," she said in a sexy tone. "You got fire! I like that. You must be Symone," she said, smiling.

"How do you know my name?" I asked.

She didn't reply.

"Who are you?" I asked, exchanging one question for another.

"I'm a businesswoman," she said sharply.

"What kind of business?"

"Public relations," she replied.

"What were you doing to that statue?" I asked her point-blank.

"What are you? The cops or something?" she asked.

"I saw you with the statue . . ."

"And?" she asked defensively.

"What were you doing to it?"

"I wasn't doing anything to the statue—" she insisted.

"But I saw you," I said, interrupting.

She rested her head against the leather seat and began to laugh out loud. It was a wild, unbridled laugh, the kind of laughing crazy people do. She may have been beautiful, but God, she was weird.

"What do you want?" I asked her straight-out.

"What do you have to give?" she asked.

"Attitude," I said.

"I'm in the market for attitude today," she said, lighting the cigarette that she was still holding in her hand. She took a puff on the cig and handed it to me.

I don't know why but I accepted and tried to imitate her smoothness. But of course I choked.

"Easy, baby," she said.

She stared ahead, speaking to me as if I weren't really there.

"I saw you checking me out," she said, smiling.

"I wasn't checking you out," I shot back, slightly embarrassed because I had been checking her out.

"You like me, don't you?" she said playfully.

"I'm just bored," I said, trying to seem disinterested though I was anything but.

I could have allowed myself to ponder a wild fantasy of her and I had I not been interrupted by Ridge Huston, who swung open the door on my side so fast I almost got whiplash spinning my head toward the sound.

"Get out of the car," he said to me harshly.

I shot eyes to him, then to her, and they both shot eyes at one another. Her face leaned toward apology and his to outrage. And then I got a strange, tingly feeling that the two of them were sleeping with one another.

Gross, I thought as I exited the car with a frown. *He's doing everybody in town.*

I went back inside the house and shut the door hard behind me. I scooted to a window and stole a peek outside. Ridge got into the car, shut the door behind him, and she rolled up the dark window. And God only knows what happened after that and maybe only God cared, because I sure didn't.

I turned two blind eyes and a couple deaf ears to the obvious affair. And I switched myself to OFF because "off" made it so much better. I didn't say it made it *okay,* it simply made it better. But I couldn't stay on "off" forever.

"Symone! Symone! Symone!" The thunderous voice was so loud my head nearly exploded. An arm of cellulite reached around, snatched me, and pulled me violently into a suffocating embrace. Chandler had arrived.

She kissed me. I kissed her back. Out of all of the people in this sick family, she was the one I most adored.

Chandler's story was tragic. She had about as much self-esteem as an anorexic turkey during Thanksgiving week. And sadly, her insecurities were validated by the condescending echoes of family.

I wanted her to win at the game of life—run for president or discover the cure for AIDS. Negotiate world peace or create a vaccination for the common cold. I wanted Chandler to be remembered, respected, but mostly I wanted her to be loved. Next to me, she was probably the world's loneliest inhabitant. Her existence was one of sadness and shame. Her face was only the shield that hid the pain which ate her alive.

No doubt she had problems and lots of them, but her resilience is what kept me coming back for more. She was as tough as the hurt and she could hang with the pain. When life kicked her in the butt and knocked her down she found no shame in crawling till she could get on her feet and walk again.

It is for this reason that I was so taken by her. Despite the pain, the shame, the hurt, the guilt, she never gave up, she just went on.

The unedited version of Chandler's biography: She carried around a lifetime of insecurities on a 268-pound, five-foot four-inch frame. Paying homage to the god of cellulite was a way of life for her. She was *huge* and her weight was killing her, literally.

Her breathing was labored. She had terrible hemorrhoids. Her legs were decorated by dreamy blue veins and her heart was taxed more heavily than Britain's wealthiest citizens.

Chandler was always dieting. Fasting. Or starving. She was best friends with Jenny Craig. She was intimate with *The Zone* and owned a considerable amount of stock in Weight Watchers.

Chandler had tried every gym in the city and probably owned most of the commercial exercise equipment this side of the Mississippi. But nothing—and I do mean *nothing*—had worked.

I had compassion for Chandler because she was taunted by the world and tormented by her own psyche to be twig-thin. She was appalled by her reflection and that's why she hadn't really looked into a mirror in years.

But amid the darkness there are always streaks of light. Her face was symmetrically perfect. Her eyes were a beautiful blue and her skin a delightful peach. The only catch to this stunning creature was that you had to be able to look beyond the fat to see the beauty, and most people just didn't have the time.

Chandler's obsession with food was frightening. On any given day she would put away two stacks of pancakes, a dozen sausages, uncountable strips of bacon, a box of grits, a loaf of bread converted to toast jammed with jelly, a dozen or so eggs, and then she'd ask, "What time is lunch?"

By the look on Teek's face, I could see he was in awe of her obesity. But it was not obvious to Chandler because she didn't know him the way I did.

Maybe I should have warned him that Chandler was a heifer but I just hadn't had the heart. I could have also said that Audrey was a slut and Huston a prick. I should have mentioned that Madeline was refined and polished on the outside, but underneath the diamonds, glitter, and platinum she wasn't shit. I also should have warned him that if he accepted the invitation for dinner, he might be sorry. Very, very sorry.

"Who is your guest?" asked Chandler.

"My boyfriend Teek," I said, spinning around to introduce him. She extended her hand; Teek accepted.

"Nice to meet you," Teek crooned.

"Likewise," Chandler responded shyly. I could tell by the way she looked at him she was smitten by his beauty.

"I can't believe he's called us for another fucking meeting!" Audrey blurted. As usual, all eyes turned her way.

"Audrey," Chandler said carefully, "we have company."

Audrey lit a cigarette and stared callously into Chandler's eyes. "What? You think he's got virgin ears? I'm sure he's heard 'the F-word' before. Just look at the company he keeps."

"Fuck you, Audrey," I said.

I had promised I would get through the day without cussing anybody out, but I also had known when I made the promise that if anybody would be cussed out, it would be Audrey.

"I knew you'd rise to the occasion," she said sarcastically. "I was waiting for the 'ghetto girl' in you to arrive."

Audrey knew how to sock it to me. She also knew "ghetto girl" comments were grounds for an automatic ass-kicking. But this was a holiday, and ass-kicking was outlawed on holidays.

I seriously considered making an exception and beating her

down anyway, but decided against traumatizing the dinner guests.

It would've been a fantastic sight to have Audrey seated at the dinner table with her plastic boobs dented inward. But that wasn't my plan for today. No, I devoted today to other plans.

CHAPTER ELEVEN

Huston's mandated meetings meant one of two things: You were going to be screwed, or you were going to be *really* screwed.

Every time Ridge Huston called a meeting we all went in wondering what we would lose by the time it was over. Would it be a crippling hit or a slight one, barely noticeable? Would it be an inconvenient scrape of the knee or an amputation of the leg? Would it be a minor cut or a full on hemorrhage?

I needed another Valium. I would down anything to numb the reality. And the reality was I *had* to be at this meeting. I would have rather stayed home and dug out my toenails with a can opener, or lain on my back and allowed scorpions to mate on my stomach, but I couldn't. Two days prior to my arrival, I had been notified by Huston's attorney that this meeting would directly impact my business, so attendance was critical and necessary. The notification made me a little nervous. No—actually, it scared the hell out of me because if there was one thing in this life that I poured myself into, it was my business.

I was part owner of a gallery I named after myself. I called the gallery *Misfits.* I purchased artwork from local artists and displayed it in the gallery. I sought unusual pieces and themes that represented the human condition. They were obscure items that could have easily been dismissed as ugly, till you looked a little closer.

A collection of headless dolls represented a nation of people who had lost their minds. The artist who created this piece had spent his life battling schizophrenia.

A sculpture of a woman whose reproductive area had been torn away by the gods, called us to accountability in the way we reproduce.

It was expensive operating Misfits so I had a business partner, Sam, and he flipped half the expenses. Sam was a retired officer of the U.S. Army and he owned a little cigar shop in my neighborhood. Back in the day, I was always in his store buying smokes, tooting about my dreams. And one day out of the blue he said, "How about a partner to get that dream of yours off the ground?"

He was old and tired so I did most of the work. But I didn't mind at all. I enjoyed the independence that having him share expenses gave me so that there was never a need for dependence on the Hustons. Out of Audrey, Chandler, and myself, I was the only one who did not have a monthly living allowance. I was too proud and too angry to take anything from the Hustons.

It was also gratifying having someone else believe in me enough to invest their money. Actually, it wasn't even that Sam believed. I think the only reason he helped support the gallery in his own words were, "You a cute girl." *Whatever, Sam.* I let him have his harmless fantasy of him and me. It kept the rent paid every month. But the concept of the gallery had not yet caught on in the city, and until it did, we struggled. But even when we came up short we always managed to make ends meet. It was funny how dreams always managed to hold themselves together, even without glue or thread.

Shortly after my arrival at the estate, Audrey, Chandler, and I gathered quietly in the sterile quarters of the conference room. Teek was left in the game room to preoccupy himself with highlights from last week's game.

Chandler found a seat in a chair that was much too small for her other side. She chomped on a bag of half-burnt popcorn, shuffled a can of soda, and battled the excess crumbs. She was oblivious and consumed by it at the same time—not the food, just the process of eating. She was chewing so fast and swallowing so hard, I can't imagine she even had time to make note of simple things like, *What am I eating? Does it have a taste?* and *Aren't I full yet?* It was ritualistic the way she ate. And it almost made me ill to watch.

Audrey tended to her makeup and admired her face and form. She was obsessive about her appearance, constantly pouting her lips into a handheld mirror. I was convinced there was a form of neurosis in the way she was always checking her profile, tilting her head backwards, scooping her bangs into the palm of her hands then sliding them through her fingers, laying them just so.

Adjusting her breasts, arching her back, patting her pants, straightening her shirt, tipping her hat, and scanning the room once over to make sure no one had forgotten to stare. This, too, was enough to make me ill as I watched.

And what about me? I sat there like a little gnat on a giant log wondering, *What the hell am I doing here this time?*

"Give it a rest, Chandler" said Audrey, annoyed. "You remind me of a zoo monkey the way you're eating that popcorn!"

"Monkeys don't eat popcorn," said Chandler, as half-chewed bits of popped corn flew from her mouth.

"What bullshit is Huston up to now?" I asked, abruptly ending their love squabble.

"Father wouldn't appreciate you calling his meetings 'bullshit,' " Audrey scolded.

"Well, if you can find a suitable replacement adjective I'll be happy to use word substitution," I replied sarcastically.

Audrey turned away in disgust, muttering under her breath, "Perhaps if you were a real Huston you would feel differently." Audrey never forgot that I didn't belong and she would never let me forget it, either, not that I ever wanted to, mind you.

The estate was nothing to be reckoned with, and the sole legal representative of all Huston's assets walked in and stood before us like a pasha surveying his harem.

Harry Fucking Comb.

"Fucking" wasn't really his middle name, but it should have been. Fucking was his occupation. He was an attorney, but not just any attorney—Ridge's attorney.

His stats: Caucasian male. Late forties. An alkie. Bad hair-plug job. He tooted around town in a sports car that screamed, *I am having a midlife crisis!* Expensive tweed suit. Cheap shoes. Nervous laugh. A married man and practicing adulterer.

He had attended the bogus family meeting to make it more official, I guess. Or he could have been there to hold up the wall. The moment I laid eyes on Comb I thought, *Damn, I should have brought extra lubricant. I'm really gonna feel it this time.*

And feel something I did, the moment the double doors slid apart and Ridge Huston entered. He was immaculately groomed inside a bold purple suit. The color was so rich and daring only two kinds of people could have pulled off a look like that, a godfather or a motherfucker.

Ridge's appearance was suave and engaging but his personality was stiff and boring. He didn't laugh too loud or move too fast. He was stingy with his smiles and choosy about whom he shook hands with.

Ridge was a sanitary freak, majorly germ-conscious. He always worried he was going to catch something from somebody.

Ridge never engaged in small talk. Conversation was not an art form in his world, it was a means to an end. A means to make more money and to end the necessity of idle chatter.

The way I saw Ridge, he was distant from reality and out of touch with the real world, real people, and real problems. He was a rich, charming, ruthless, egotistical businessman. All the stuff American dreams are made of, the wealthy bastard.

He walked into the room without grand production, exchanging hands with Comb and looks with us. He stood beside Comb, dead center of the room, and if you didn't know better, you might have even called him "handsome." It would be effortless to be taken in by his firm physique aging so well, salt-and-pepper hair so beautifully styled, and learned elegance. But if you knew better you would know his presence was a statement all its own. It dictated that he was king of the jungle, ruler of the nation. And we were little more than meager subjects without a voice, a vote, or a chance. His presence dictated power and the intensity of our oppression.

"Good afternoon," said Huston in his serious voice.

Yep, *serious* meant we were screwed.

"I have some concerns about the future. And with that in mind I have spent the past several weeks evaluating my estate. And at my discretion the will has been altered."

Someone gasped. The outburst was not my own so I glanced

around the room to see who was preparing to faint, and of course it was Audrey. She sat rigid in her chair, trembling and speechless.

The only thing in life Audrey really cared about was her inheritance. And in the end it didn't matter what you did just so long as you didn't touch the cash.

"What's the bottom line?" I asked, irritated as hell.

"In legal terms . . ." Huston hedged.

"We don't need legal terms. We're all prepared for the big screw," I interrupted.

"Give it to us straight," added Chandler.

Huston mopped his brow and began, "Audrey . . ."

I turned to the raving beauty and it was just as I thought. She was as pale as a vampire and had gone so long without taking a breath, brain damage was imminent. There was a quiet stir in the room or a pause that ran too long.

"You have a degree from a good university but you don't put it to use. As a matter of fact, you seem blissfully disinterested in making a contribution toward your livelihood. It sickens me to watch you give in to a life of sexual escapades without discretion or morality. You are not the child I raised you to be, Audrey. And with that, you leave me no choice but to cut you from the will. In the event of my demise, the provisions from my estate that I have left you with are *none*. And effective immediately your monthly living allowance is suspended."

I didn't see the look on Audrey's face, but then again, how could I? Before Huston could deliver the final blow she was flat on her face on the floor.

No one rushed to her aid because the nutty chick was known for her ability to stop breathing and pass out at a moment's notice.

"Why? Why?" Audrey cried, coming back to life. "Why are you doing this to me!"

No one answered because nobody cared. The Hustons could be called many things, but compassionate was not one of them.

After a moment of silence Ridge continued. "And Chandler, you are one of my biggest disappointments. Your weight is so out of control I don't even know where to begin. Have you no shame for your gluttony?" he asked, shaking his head. "I can't save you if you insist on eating yourself to death. I am so saddened by the direction your life has taken. You leave me no choice but to remove you from the will, and in the event of my death the provisions I have left for you are *none*. Your monthly allowance has also been suspended."

Chandler didn't say a word. But the water that swelled in her eyes told the whole story.

Huston stood the entire time with Comb by his side, engaged in the titillating pleasure that cutting us from his will brought him.

He had already stabbed Chandler in the center of her heart and left Audrey for dead facedown on the floor. I sat back patiently and waited for the eleventh hour, because it was then I knew he would rush in and destroy the wounded.

"And last but not least," said Huston as he savored the moment, "Symone. My disappointment in you takes this all to another level. You glorify a life of sexual dysfunction, consumed by your attraction toward women when I know I taught you better than that. Perhaps you've managed to be discreet, but you've failed to remember that I have eyes all around me and they read between the lines. You've disgraced me and made a mockery of our family name. You have no respect for what it means to be a Huston. And if I died tomorrow, you wouldn't see a penny of the Huston fortune. Not a cent," he repeated bitterly.

Yet again the room went still and no one said a word. Audrey was on the floor. Chandler sobbed quietly. And I sat there like the fool I was for showing up again. And again. And again, called to this place like unresolved karma, coming back to rewrite a wrong story and make it right again, not that it ever was right, may I remind you.

"So, let's recap," I said sarcastically. "You invited us here today to say that we're cut out of your will because Audrey's a slut, Chandler's fat, and I'm bisexual?"

"My decision runs deeper than all of those reasons combined," Huston snapped. "None of you represent the Huston legacy with dignity and honor."

"How dare you!" I challenged.

"Symone . . . ," warned Chandler.

"How dare you," I said, my voice low and hollow. "What do you know about honor?"

"I suggest you gather yourself, Symone," Ridge Huston said strongly. "I'm not done yet. Your gallery, Misfits, has been of interest to me for some time now. I have made a very generous offer to your partner, Samuel Wellington, to buy out his half of the business. Wellington agreed to the terms and the deal was consummated two days ago. So congratulations, looks like I'm your new partner," he said with a subtle, evil grin.

Partner?

My gallery?

Now part "your" gallery?

Our gallery?

It hit me hard, the words. Like the force of a 747 crashing against the runway with the landing gear gone and the belly filled with fuel.

I was blown to bits, one piece at a time. Gravediggers had just dug out my heart and thrown it in the trenches like a useless piece of meat. I needed that heart to keep beating, moving, and shaking. Huston had just sucked the wind from my wings and life from my body. I wanted to die, or better yet, kill someone. How could a dream that was so definitively *mine* be stolen by someone else? And not just anyone, but the one who had taken so much already? The gallery was mine. It belonged to me, separate from the Huston name and tradition. I had built the gallery on long hours, sweat, blood, and passion. *Not everything is for sale. Goddamn you, Sam.* It was a small piece of the world I had carved for myself. It was the only confirmation I had that I was sane instead of crazy, alive instead of existing, and healing instead of dying from the wound.

It was mine.

Huston didn't buy out my partner because he cared so much about the gallery, the work inside of it, or what it represented to my soul. He bought out Sam because it was the only way he could fuck me without laying me down.

All of the breathable air in the room suddenly dried up and I was unclear of my options. I looked into Chandler's eyes and saw she was as close to death as I was.

We didn't exchange words but then again we didn't have to. We had both danced on top of the same hot coals and once again we mourned together because we knew it was our very lives that were killing us.

"Just let it go," said Chandler, her tone desperate. "You're only going to make it worse for us."

"Make it worse!" I said, turning to face her. How could I possibly make it worse? How could I make hell hotter? How could I make the evil we saw or were about to become more ugly? Or more wicked?

I love you, Chandler, I thought to myself. *God knows I do, but sometimes you are brilliantly naïve.* "How could I possibly make it any worse?"

"Audrey? Audrey?" cried Chandler.

Audrey was still facedown on the floor, damaged. Chandler pulled herself from the chair and got down on all fours to check on her. I had little interest in Audrey's vitals so I found it difficult to participate in this exercise.

"Chandler, please get off the floor," I said. Chandler was weak, too weak to scour the floor searching for signs of life from the greediest bitch in town.

I loved Chandler deeply but found it challenging to care for Audrey. It wasn't that I didn't love Audrey. I did love her, just found it piercingly difficult to *like* her.

I rose to my feet. It was time to gather Teek and get the hell out. I tried to assist Chandler in standing but she resisted, too consumed by drama as both she and Audrey sobbed pitifully. I let her be and made swift tracks toward the door until I was stopped by a familiar voice.

"I wouldn't do it," she said sternly.

I knew the voice too well.

"Don't walk," she reaffirmed.

I turned toward the voice only to behold Her Majesty in full glory. Madeline had finally arrived. She had slipped into the conference room on the pulse of commotion only to find herself upstaged by the theatrics of her children.

The diva was extraordinarily beautiful today. She was elegant and poised, displaying a look I might actually admire if I weren't so distracted by my anger. Her makeup was flawless and her eyes so clear they looked to be liquid-filled. Perhaps these were her tears.

"Symone, sit down," she said in a hollow tone.

And I did. I don't know why but I did.

"Get up, Audrey, Chandler. Pull yourselves together and stop being so dramatic," Madeline snapped, litigating organization.

Chandler, with the help of Audrey, Comb, and Madeline, was vertical again. Audrey sat down in the chair and Comb stood silently against the wall.

"These alterations to my will are temporary," Ridge inserted as if that statement was supposed to strengthen the rickety bridge over troubled waters. "And they will be modified once you have complied with my wishes."

His wishes meant living life on his terms and not on your own. It meant following orders and crawling around on your knees waiting for him to penetrate thoughts into your head before you were even allowed to think.

"Who do you think you are?" I found myself asking him out loud. Madeline's face twisted with displeasure. *No talking back, little rat,* I could almost hear her whisper.

I could not stand to look at these demons any longer so I headed for the door again, determined this time to get out.

"As your new business partner, I believe it would be in your best interest to stay through dinner," Huston admonished. "After all, I would like to discuss the new arrangements of the gallery with you."

New arrangements?

I could feel Huston climbing all over me. I could feel his skin, sweat, blood, and the prickly edge of his tongue. I could feel hot air leaking from his nostrils, singeing me.

"The Mercedes payment is due next week," said Audrey desperately. "Will that be covered?"

There were no answers, only silence.

Audrey took in a long deep breath. She knew there would be no answers till Ridge gave them and even Madeline couldn't tell us when that would happen.

"I just can't believe it," mumbled Chandler.

"We're going to have a lovely dinner this evening," said Madeline, interrupting everybody's emotions. "I'm serving an exotic bird with elaborate trimmings and fabulous pastries."

Excuse me, but does anyone give a shit about a turkey dinner right now?

CHAPTER TWELVE

Following the meeting, I found myself standing in the backdraft of a hallway where I began remembering what I never could forget.

It was time.

Time to disrupt *agony* and summon it from its resting place. I was about to open the book on a tale I so desperately needed to forget.

I shall lay it out, the truth, in bits and pieces. Bits and pieces are all I can do until I complete the search of my emotional wreckage for the answers.

This is where ugly was born.

Though the Hustons had legally adopted me, I was not their child by birthright. This caused dissension among the progenitors. When I was growing up, they treated me like a science project. I was put through the rigors of Huston training. Madeline used to say, "You may not have our blood, but you've got our breeding and that's just as good."

Madeline was dogmatic about my relationship with standard American English. And she saw to it that I had no detectable African-American accent. In other words, they didn't want me to sound like the black girl I was at heart.

By the age of fourteen I had gone from the illiteracy to the honor roll. I was upgraded from a "project girl" to a prima donna. I had every material comfort the world could suggest and my basic needs were met one-thousandfold. Life in Dorchester was only a memory and it appeared I'd caught the last star as it fell down from the heavens.

I had grown into a beautiful woman.

My breasts peeked out and parked themselves boldly up front. My ass was perfectly round and extended, offering a little something to hold on to. My hips did a dip, a flip, and a curve. My legs made a statement all their own.

My last bout with puberty left me in my mother's image. My African-American features slid in through the window that was so rudely labeled BLACKS ONLY. Childhood was fading fast and womanhood was screaming my name. My bright skin mellowed to a beautiful caramel and the blond hair trickled down to brown. My blue, blue eyes faded to gray. Ignoramuses called me "mulatto" and educated fools referred to me as "biracial."

I no longer subscribed to the Caucasian world because it was clear that my African heritage had awakened and pushed its way to the front of the bus. And from the looks of things, my blackness had taken out a long-term lease and would be staying around awhile.

But I struggled to keep my beauty a disguise because I was shy about my womanhood, my breasts and curves, my dips and hips. Adolescence felt shameful at times. Why was it happening to *me?* I hid my breasts and buried my behind in bulky clothes. I negated makeup and steered clear of cosmetic enhancement.

In the eyes of a stranger I was the luckiest girl in town. A poor niggah girl, light enough to pass for white, bought out by a wealthy family. Dorchester girls would have died to take my place and I would have been willing to kill myself to give it up.

I used to sit on the balcony of my imported Italian bedroom, staring at the pool decorated by rose petals. I could see the tennis courts, which barely hid the golf course. This was merely an extension of the vineyard where the lake ran and dipped into the waterfalls, which decorated the estate. And still I longed for the ghetto.

I missed the common man.

The blue-collar worker.

The ordinary people.

Gladys.

Gladys was a snappy-dressing, loud-talking, overbearing, lop-sided, Afro-wearing, single mother of four big-headed boys. Every morning you'd see her marching those bad-ass kids off to school. They marched single file and in silence. If one of her demon sons got out of line, Gladys would slap the shit out of him. Gladys said she was teaching her kids discipline and respect. I don't know if they ever learned discipline or respect but they could march till the cows came home.

Gladys's last name was Mitchell and I used to say to Dolores when I saw them coming, "Here comes the Mitchell parade."

I also missed the one-legged bum, Joe. He lived on the street. His bed was the hard, cold, filthy, urine-stained sidewalk. The neighborhood kids stepped on Joe's bed every day.

Joe slept with one eye open because the last time he closed both at the same time somebody jumped him. People used to do nasty stuff to Joe at night when he slept. They did less when he kept one eye open.

Most of the people in the neighborhood made fun of Joe. The boys mocked his hobble and the girls threw nasty looks. But me, I just felt sorry for him. I used to tell myself, *Must be fucked up being Joe.*

Joe was desperate for cash but he never asked me for a dime. I used to bring him a cup of hot water every morning so he could warm up. When we had extra money I made Dolores buy coffee so I could make a cup for Joe.

If you looked at Joe, you'd probably get sick to your stomach. He was disgusting, unkempt, filthy, and way funky. But if you really looked you could see he used to be handsome.

Joe was nobody. But if you stuck around long enough to have a conversation, you'd realize he was *somebody*.

Joe's luck ran out the day he was crippled by a car accident. He lost his job. His home. His wife. His kids. Even the mutt he saved from death row at the local pound took a hike. Joe's world was cut off, just like his leg.

He was a company man. A "yes sir, no sir" man. Some called him a "house niggah" or a token for the white man. But none of that mattered by the time I met Joe because he was a homeless man.

Nobody gave a damn about his past, present, or future. When people saw Joe, they didn't look at him as a man, or a human, for that matter. He was just a nameless face in a sea of people you just didn't want to see.

One morning on my way to school I stopped and gave Joe his usual cup of hot water.

"Thank you, girl," he said smiling, missing most of his teeth. "You sure are good to me," he said, slowly sipping the hot water.

"No coffee today, Joe," I said. "Just water."

"That's okay, girl. It don't bother Joe none. If I close my eyes real hard when I drink, it tastes just like coffee."

When I heard Joe say he could turn water into coffee, my eyes did a dance in my head. I could just imagine what I might do with Dolores's stale-ass Kool-Aid. I spent the rest of that year trying to change water into soda.

It wasn't till later in life that I realized Joe was fooling with me. I must have given myself a dozen nosebleeds from thinking so hard. And the frustration of it all, no matter how hard I thought, wished, or dreamed, was that I was still only drinking rusty, stinking water with flavored sugar powder.

It was on the same morning Joe tricked me about the mind thing that I had my very first real conversation with him.

After I could see he was starting to open up, I decided to take the talk to the next level.

"Why you never ask me for money, Joe?" I asked. "I know you need money."

Joe's expression dropped to a scary, serious one; I was so frightened by his face I wanted to take it back. But it was too late. He just sat there on the ground looking pitiful and rejected.

"I don't borrow from friends. That's the quickest way to end up friendless. And besides, if I asked you for money you might mistake me for a bum."

But you are a bum! I wanted to say, but didn't have the heart. So at that point I decided to make Joe my friend.

Joe was symbolic of life, the life I was missing.

I missed the hustlers, dreamers, thinkers, and schemers. I missed people lining up for lottery tickets and 'hood rats crowding in cold alleys to keep warm. I missed single mothers cussing out the welfare office because their checks were late again. I missed the know-nothing shit people used to talk on street corners and inside illegal pool halls.

I missed sitting in front of our big picture window in the living room, watching our neighbor Elly tell lies to her husband Rufus about why another man's drawers came out in the wash. Everybody on the block knew Elly was a slut. Everybody knew but Rufus.

It was hard to tell where reality ended and where my life began and ended. On the outside I was a Huston, love child of a family fortune. On the inside I was a ghetto girl with fading blond hair and changing blue eyes.

Now I will tell you what happened, when it happened, and every detail that I can bear to put on the page.

Just before my mother's body erupted through my own skin, somewhere between the sunrise of womanhood and the sunset of adolescence, I was raped. I was violently raped again and again.

The journey did not begin that way but, unfortunately, it was the destination. As a survivor I have learned there is no middle ground when it comes to molestation. It will do either one of two things: break you in half *or*, under more merciful conditions, it will leave you in one piece with a giant hole blown from your center. You either survive or you don't.

Survivors don't survive by accident. They do it because they resolve to do so. They *refuse* to lie down and become part of the dust.

The journey to survival is a bitch.

But first . . .

I was twelve when I woke up one day and saw breasts where there had been only bumps. A butt extended from where there had only been a flat backside with a split in it. I saw hips where there had only been long scrawny legs, and meat where there had only been bone.

Womanhood was conflicting with my adolescent agenda but there was no turning back.

I undressed myself only to notice stubs of hair growing between my legs and in the off-limits crack area of my rear end. What was going on here? There was also the eruption of annoying fuzz underneath my arms.

I summoned a razor and shaved myself bare, but that was only to my dismay because it grew back a few days later, with itching vengeance.

Everyone in the Huston family noticed I had sprouted. I was tormented with jokes from Audrey and Chandler. Even Madeline managed to comment here and there. Ridge was silent, but then again, he always was. I had no idea that he'd even noticed my budding body till the following weekend.

It was Saturday night, a lost fall evening. Outside, the wind ripped with chill but the inside offered non-discriminating warmth.

Madeline had taken Audrey and Chandler to modeling school, their absence leaving me home alone with Ridge Huston. This was not unusual. I had been alone with him on many occasions. After all, I hated modeling and never wanted to accompany the Three Stooges to the studio.

I never did have much contact with Ridge, as he stayed on his wing of the mansion, and I on mine. Except lately—I remembered in recent weeks that every time I was present, he had been attentive. Every time I spoke, he responded. Every time I wanted, he was there to give. So much was he in my face, that I feared one morning I would awake to take my morning shit and find him conveniently stationed in the Tidy Bowl, ready to wipe my ass. But on this particular night he invited me downstairs to the formal dining room after everyone had left. I accepted the invite, but with caution, because it was so unusual.

When I entered the room, candles were lit and sober music echoed off bland walls. An ensemble of food sat on the table and two elegant place-settings were waiting patiently for our arrival.

I sat. Huston sat.

Silence.

He smiled. I almost smiled but couldn't.

Silence.

He winked. I looked away.

He poured himself a glass of wine and poured me one as well. I wouldn't have thought much of this, but I was only twelve years old. He toasted, raising glasses to the sky offering two simple words: "To us."

I suddenly felt an extrasensory chill giving me a subtle message—*Get out NOW!*

I tried to keep it together on the outside; cool. But on the inside my heart perspired and stuck between beats, pounding erratically. I thought it would surely tear through my chest, leap onto the table, and break into song.

For the first time, Ridge Huston actually looked at me. His eyes danced from the floor to the ceiling and made an emergency landing on my breasts, a second landing on my crotch, and a third into my eyes, and then through me.

His blue eyes were glazed and his face was a surreal scarlet color.

He wouldn't take his eyes off me.

He studied, observed, and dissected me.

I sat consumed with anxiety as I asked myself the abhorrent question, *Is he seducing me?*

Though it felt absurd, it didn't sound so crazy. I was adopted, not a blood relative. I feared the sneaky bastard who spent the past several years ignoring this little girl, had suddenly found himself drawn to the woman I had become overnight.

I knew the only way to discover what was really going on was to look between his legs. And so I waited. I waited for an opportune time to check his privates. I would wait till he stood and all truths would be told. And sooner than I wanted, he got up and stepped across the room to adjust the thermostat.

I stole a peek.

And there it stood.

The enemy, an explosive, throbbing erection bulging through the crotch of his trousers.

In horror I turned away, but he caught my stare at a compromising moment, and it was then I knew it was just too late.

Huston grabbed me without warning and threw me on the floor. I struggled intensely but my strength was no match for his. He was all-consuming and powerful as he gripped me in a headlock. He then reached his hands between my legs and forced them apart. Before I could gasp for air, he was sliding on top of me and had already penetrated me halfway. How this had happened so quickly was still a blur to me. I was fighting so hard but losing so fast.

I heard sounds of moaning as he continued to thrust himself farther inside, all the while forcing my legs apart as if trying to break me in two. As he shoved himself deeper into me, I felt my hymen rupture. Whether it was a quick snap, a mini-tear, or an exaggerated stretching, I don't remember. But what I do remember is, it hurt. It hurt like hell.

I cried out in pain as Huston began to push deeper inside of me. And after what seemed an eternity, he made one more single, violent thrust, followed by a deep moan. And then he slowed down to a stop.

He grabbed my face and kissed me, forcing his tongue deep inside my mouth, which only made him harder on top of me.

He put his arms around me in what appeared to be an embrace until I realized this was no hug. It was an attempt to suffocate me. My eyes widened in panic but he did not let go. At that moment, he applied so much pressure the veins in his head begin to protrude through the skin. His face turned a dusty red and his pupils dilated against the deepness of his face.

He was trying to kill me, and that much I was certain of.

Not only had he just stripped me of the only dignity I had ever known, now he was going to finish me off with a kiss followed by strangulation.

I tried to push him off, but couldn't. But the moment all oxygen ceased to flow to my brain, I became energized by adrenaline. I lifted my upper body, forcing Huston to fall off and slam onto his back.

Like a wild, raging animal I leapt to my knees, gasping for air.

I choked.

Gagged.

Cried.

And cried out.

Huston lay doubled over on the floor, writhing in pain. It appeared my left knee had slammed into his penis during the encounter.

It was possible Huston was trying to regroup so that he could finish me off, but not before bright headlights shone through the window. He immediately aborted plans for my execution and stood up without hesitation.

"Get up! Get up!" he shouted. "Someone's here!"

I jumped up and grabbed my clothes, holding them desperately to my naked, bruised flesh.

"If you tell anyone—I mean *anyone*—we will finish our business in hell," he said as his eyes turned a cold, glazed black.

Of course I consented, swearing not to tell. I promised to keep it all inside and allow it to slowly eat me away, from the inside out. It would be a slow, agonizing death but it would be easier than a public declaration of a very private rape.

I ran out of the room, fleeing to my bedroom for safety. I got tangled at least three times in the necessities I carried, things that should have protected me, saved me. Things like a training bra, panties, pants, and a shirt.

Once inside my room, I pressed myself against the door to keep out the demons. As I stood horrified by what had just happened, my trembling and shaken body felt the wetness of Huston's sperm as it did a slow crawl down my legs. And it was then I literally wanted to release myself from my skin and come undone.

I was exhausted. My body was frosted and riddled with pain, in desperate need to nurse tears along the edge of my rectum and reduce the enlarged membranes of a swollen vagina.

I was too consumed by fear and disbelief to comprehend what had just happened to me. I was too racked by hysteria to talk myself back to sanity.

I couldn't believe Ridge Huston had gone stark raving mad just before the midnight hour in the twelfth year and third month and seventeenth day and the tenth hour of my existence. He stole all that would be mine forever and shoved it in his back pocket like a pack of bubble gum.

This was no misunderstanding.

No miscommunication.

No enticements, no lure or allure for that matter, between us.

It wasn't like his penis "accidentally" slipped out of his pants and fell into my private areas by happenstance.

It wasn't like he could actually say, *Sorry, I seem to have misplaced my manhood. Oh, here it is . . . conveniently placed inside your vagina. Pardon me while I remove it. Oh, and if by chance I shatter you in the process, please forgive me for that as well. I just felt compelled to indulge myself today in recreational, hedonistic sickness.*

He had gone from gentleman to animal and through his degeneracy; the real story was born.

He had fooled the world, and perhaps the world should have been fooled. It was filled with idiots who glorified him simply because of his wealth and power. But little did they know his flesh and bone were merely a disguise. The blood pumping through his veins was merely access to the human race. And though he probably did possess a beating heart, this certainly did not qualify him the dignity to be called human.

A part of me couldn't remember what had just happened but a greater part of me would never forget.

I was numb, yet at the same time there was a gaping wound with all senses heightened, and I was prepared to defend myself to the death.

Through a distant window I saw the shining headlights that had just saved my life came from a car that had made a wrong turn. The car had used the driveway for a quick turn around.

No one was here.

No one was coming.

And no one would ever come again.

I reassembled what was left of my sanity and drew a bath.

I wanted to bathe in the dark but found that when the lights went down my anxiety soared. When I tried a second time to turn out the lights, I began to suffocate. It was a slow, mute strangulation that danced against my being. It lay against me like a cement block, pressing against my abdomen, slowly moving in an upward direction against my windpipe.

It was then I knew there would be no darkness tonight.

I soaked for two, maybe three hours. I rubbed and scrubbed till my skin cracked and nearly bled. I ached all over as the bruises began to light up and the welts swelled against my skin. My throat was on fire and my vagina was so torn that I would have to put on a sanitary pad.

As I drowned my ravaged flesh in the tub I knew this was the darkest day of my life.

To my disgust, through the vents I could hear Ridge Huston having sex with Madeline later that night.

Madeline moaned like it was the first time. I could also hear the all-too-familiar sound of Huston as he pleasured himself for yet a second time that night.

I pulled my lifeless body from the tub and stood naked in the center of the floor. It was probably forty degrees in the drafty bathroom but I didn't bother reaching for a towel.

I had bigger worries than catching a chill or pneumonia.

I had greater issues than the black and blue that covered my body.

My thoughts went beyond the handprints on my neck or the loss of oxygen and possible brain damage I had sustained from this experience.

I'd even take a leap beyond the confusion, horror, pain, hurt, guilt, shame, and silence. And even if you do the two-step around the innocence I had just lost, remember this: I woke up a virgin. I went to bed a rape victim.

What else is there?

CHAPTER THIRTEEN

And for more than a decade there has been nothing else. In my sleep I remember. In my waking hours I can't forget. In my leisure I am tormented. In the middle of laughter I break into sobs without warning. My good moods turn sour without justification and in the midst of my tears, I dim to stoicism because I can't deal with the inconvenience of my past. Huston penetrated more than my vaginal walls. He punctured my soul.

"Are you okay?" asked Teek as he leaned into me. After the meeting, we had returned to the inn to rest a few hours before dinner.

"I need to lay down," I said, half out of my mind, half in it. I hadn't told Teek about Huston's hostile takeover of my gallery. I wasn't prepared to talk about it yet, not that I ever would be, but eventually I would—talk about it, that is.

"Baby, are you okay?" he repeated.

"Fine," I said, facing off with the lie. No, I wasn't okay but I couldn't tell him that. I had been brought to the Huston palace, treated like a queen in public, raped like an animal in private, paid off like a whore between the lines, and left for dead as an adult.

No. I wasn't okay.

I could've done a line of coke. Made love to Teek on top of the table. Beat the shit out of Audrey just because. Purchased a high-powered weapon. Blown Huston's head off the first chance I got. Hung his decapitated face in my gallery as restored junk, got to bed by nine, and slept like a baby through the night.

Did I sound okay?

Teek reached around my waist and pulled me to him. I always got the chills when he did that because my waist was the most sensitive area on my body.

"I want to be with you," I said to him, disengaging mind from body. And that was all I had to say. It would only take a moment for him to oblige. He laid me down on the bed and stood over me . . .

Undressing.

Revealing.

Disarming.

"You are so beautiful," I said, admiring him.

He slowly undressed me.

Slowly.

It was almost sweet, the seduction. But Teek was not big on foreplay and before I had a chance to remember that my childhood was over he had already penetrated me.

Okay.

Okay.

Okay.

He's inside again.

He's touching and moving and groping and stealing things that don't belong to him. He has taken things not due him. He has purchased goods that weren't for sale and put a price on innocence.

"Oh," he moaned. "So good, baby . . . it's so good," he said again.

Okay.

Okay.

It's just my body, it's not my soul. Just my body, not my soul. He can't touch me. He can't really get inside me.

"You smell so good," he whispered in my ear.

"Come," I said aloud.

"Oooohhh . . ." he bellowed.

"Come," I said again.

Come and I will blow your head off. Come and die. Come and die.

"Symone," he moaned.

"Come," I said again with no emotion.

Abigail, where are you? I could feel my heart begging for her—the Messiah I created long ago. *Abigail, have you slipped into the night and condensed yourself from fantasy to nonexistence? Has the city of deaf-mutes consumed you? And why have you not come to save me yet? I always thought you would come.*

I could feel the engorgement of my vagina as I accidentally slipped away on an orgasm.

As I came, I envisioned Huston's head separating from his body and his whole existence exploding into thousands of pieces.

"Ooooohhhhh," I moaned.

"I'm . . . I'm . . ." groaned Teek. *About to come? I don't think so.* He didn't have time. I snapped, went berserk, pushed him off me, and tried to fight back. I kicked, clawed, screamed, and howled. Teek quickly dismounted and backed against the wall with his hands in the air.

He knew the look. He had seen it before. The look was the storm, the last breath before death. The clock was wound and the bomb set.

"Symone," he called out, trying to bring me back. "Symone!" he called again, but this time I heard him. When I realized it was Teek, I stopped the assault and came back to mind and body. I was safe now. Huston was done for the night.

I started to cry. Every once in a while when I made love to Teek I felt Huston inside of me. And I felt so helpless, unable to exit the figurative penetration by someone who wasn't there, or was he? It was the familiar sensation of skin against skin caressing me like sandpaper. I loathed it and at the same I felt ashamed because I had not yet been able to outrun my past.

"Baby," he whispered, bent with confusion, trying to decide if he should come close or stay away. I was so unpredictable at times, a stranger to myself. The outbursts were my attempt to try and save myself from perceived danger, a fight or flight response, I guess.

"I can't breathe, Teek," I said in a barely audible voice.

He looked as frightened as I was but said nothing. There was still no proper explanation for all of the things that had been done in the dark.

"I got scared . . . that's all," I said, lowering my head, scurrying to justify my madness and to excuse it. He knelt beside me and stroked my hair. He was so tender and in looking into his eyes I found compassion.

"You're beautiful to me," I said.

It was hard to move beyond his exterior beauty because rarely is perfection so graciously distributed on mortals. But in his case, Mother Nature was competing against herself for a masterpiece.

"So beautiful . . . ," I said again, because it was honest and raw and real.

He wrapped his body around mine in an embrace that was so powerful, I knew it was for moments like this I always came back, delivering myself temporarily from the haunting of my past. I came back because his love was authentic and proper and the only validation that I was at the very least human.

Teek had always been very patient with me sexually. He never knew why I did the things I did but he knew there were reasons. And I believe he stayed because he knew one day I would share them with him, the reasons.

He was a martyr for love, wanting to see our love through, regardless of the consequence. He always said I was his "beautiful moon with crimson highlights." And it would have been too difficult for him to walk away from such a beautiful creature, painfully tainted or not. Maybe the only reason Teek stayed was because he was as twisted as I was and we just never talked about it. The question of the hour: *Why did he stay?* The answer of the moment: *Why does anyone stay?*

"Why do you stay with me?" I asked, because I simply had to know. He didn't answer so I pushed it further: "Why do you stay?"

He looked down and paused a beat and simply said, "Don't know."

"No?" I asked.

"No," he reaffirmed.

"I don't like your answer," I said tersely.

"I don't like your question," he shot back.

"Do you know why I think you stay?" I asked him.

"Why?" He put it back on me with one brow raised.

"You have nowhere else to go," I said flatly. "Do you know why I stay?" I asked him.

He shook his head.

"I have nowhere else to go," I said, dropping into silence. He smiled, then reassured me of at least minimal fondness with a gentle kiss upon the forehead. And for the moment that was enough. But moments have a way of deceiving the ones to whom they belong.

I knew I couldn't live this way anymore. I wanted Ridge Huston dead. My bitter soul whispered to me that my next orgasm would be his execution. And not only had I heard it, I was eager to respond.

Huston kept guns in the house and I knew this. He had an entire room filled with them. If I could get my hands on one, I would end the suffering for good. There would never be a need to return for Band-Aids that never fit or mend a past that never healed.

Teek and I lay down on the bed and he held me in his arms. The moment was tranquil and still. Yet never underestimate the deception of the moment because internally I raged out of control, desperate to retard the stirring within. But what if I couldn't? What if it was already too late? I wasn't always able to disarm it and get a grip on myself. If I could stop it in time, then Ridge Huston would live to see another day. If I couldn't . . .

We would all be dining with the Devil by dinnertime.

CHAPTER FOURTEEN

The table was set. The candles were lit, the linen pristine and the atmosphere glowing. Family members were seated opposite one another, pitted against each other like pit bulls. All were present, with the exception of Huston. He always made an entrance.

Madeline sipped wine, looking as poised and fake as ever. She had exchanged her earlier, conservative dress for a more seductive number with lace and a plunging neckline.

Chandler pawed over her food, fighting back the urge to inhale it before onlookers.

Huston had invited Comb to stay through dinner and he had disappeared into his own world, getting wasted on vodka shots.

Audrey was still dazed by the blow of Huston's meeting. And

Teek sat beside me, enveloped in a blanket of mystification as to what was really going on in my world.

And me? I was starting to feel the suffocation I had felt so many nights in this arena. I was seething with resentment, trapped in growing hysteria. For I knew the sun would set with me inside the estate and I would have to devise a way to escape under the umbrella of a pitch-black sky.

Huston had won again.

He always did.

And perhaps he always would.

The angst was too much. I snatched Teek's hand, prompting him to stand with me. Suddenly, all activity ceased and the table turned their attention toward us.

"Dear, we're just about to start," said Madeline, stopping short of a reprimand.

"What's going on, Symone?" asked Chandler.

"I need a minute," I said sternly.

"For what?" asked Madeline. "What is so important that you both need to be excused from the dinner table?"

"I just need a minute," I repeated firmly, hoping she would drop it. Praying she wouldn't press me, stress me.

"A minute for what?" she asked, digging into my spine with that tone. She was starting to gnaw at my nerves.

I didn't have time for small talk. I didn't have time to comfort the wounded, console the damned, or redeem the pathetic. I just needed a minute.

I led Teek by the hand through the double doors and around the winding hallway. We quickly ducked into one of the guest bathrooms. I pulled Teek inside and closed the door almost all the way.

I ripped off my shirt and dropped my jeans.

I leaned against the marble sink, which was surrounded by mirrors.

Teek couldn't drop his jeans fast enough. I stood mesmerized by his beautiful body cut through the middle with muscle and bone.

I didn't even give him time to introduce his erect penis to me before grabbing it with both hands, dropping to my knees, eagerly anticipating meeting its head with the tip of my tongue.

I didn't have frivolous moments to waste on foreplay. And like the savage I was, I nearly swallowed his erection whole. Never mind that I was starting to gag and choke on his manhood. And disregard the fact that I was crushing my windpipe with his cumbersome dick.

I knew if he was going to calm the beast within we would have to do it fast. I needed to lay him down, envelop his body with mine. I ached to pour myself out and soak up his sanity. I longed to control it. We had to try again and Teek understood that. He grabbed me and, squeezing tight with both arms, threw me on the counter. I was so turned on that I moaned out loud, even before I had a reason to. And that's when he pushed me, slamming my body against its naked reflection in the mirror. Immediately I threw up both hands, surrendering. That's when he leaned close and penetrated me. Shortly after his first thrust I felt myself starting to go into meltdown.

Again.

My skin dewed with perspiration. My limbs went numb and my body stiff. I felt my breath slip away and I could only grab air in spurts. I felt a heavy hand on my bare neck sucking the life from my body. I was suffocating again in the dark.

And again.

And again.

I grabbed Teek's beautiful back and dug my nails into his bare skin. This wasn't the first time I had clawed him. Sometimes I drew blood and other times I didn't. His back bore many scars. Some were fading, others permanent. It was never my intention to hurt Teek, but sometimes I did.

One evening last summer while making love, I had grabbed a nearby table lamp and coldcocked him. After the unfortunate incident, Teek couldn't achieve an erection for months. Perhaps the twelve stitches just above his right eye had served as a constant reminder of how dangerous an erection could be.

But after the table-lamp incident, he drew the line and decided to leave. He came home from the emergency room that night and packed his bags.

"I can't deal with the insanity anymore," I remember him saying.

I stood in the center of the room and watched him toss all of his earthly possessions into an overnight bag. He zipped the bag closed with such finality that I felt as if he were cutting off my oxygen.

He opened the door.

Stepped out of the house.

And out of my life.

When there was nothing left in the room but silence I became terrified.

I listened to the moans of an empty house as it whispered, *You're all alone now!*

Sure, Teek was lazy. Sure, Teek was broke. He was probably a weak partner by most people's standards, but Teek loved me. Natalie had also loved me, but not as deeply as Teek. And I needed to be loved—deeply loved.

I may have been mistaken as cast iron on the exterior, but the interior was damaged, brittle, and exposed. And the truth was,

I could not live without him. And that was the biggest difference between my relationships with Teek and Natalie. Natalie was important, but Teek, he was essential.

And I was terrified of my dependency on his love. I didn't want him to leave but I would certainly understand it if he left.

After all, who would want to stay with a woman so wacked that everyday lovemaking came with a warning?—MAKING LOVE TO HER COULD BE HAZARDOUS TO YOUR HEALTH.

I knew if I let Teek get to the end of the street and make that right onto Lincoln, I would never see him again. It would be as if he never existed. If I lost sight of him it would be the last time I laid eyes on him.

But in the same breath I was a proud woman.

I was proud as hell.

And I wasn't about to go running through the street half-naked to beg some broke-ass mother to come back and let me spend my last dime on him.

"Good riddance," I whispered under my breath, dancing around tears and bullshitting with fears.

"I'm over it already," I said as I turned away.

But no sooner had I taken one step back, than I ripped open the door and went blazing down the street, wearing a pair of red flannel pajamas and a pair of flipper houseshoes.

I cut through the air, screaming his name: "Teek! Teek! Teek!" The neighbors may have been looking but I felt no shame. I caught him just as he turned onto Lincoln, and tackled him, sending him crashing to the ground. And I sat on his stomach to hold him there for safekeeping, so he wouldn't get away. And then I started to cry. I didn't want to, but the tears were so heavy I just couldn't hold them anymore.

I would imagine he had been embarrassed by the whole fiasco. A snot-nosed woman in hysterics throwing herself on top of a grown man in the middle of a public street begging him to come back. But I didn't care, just as I had not cared about many things in my life.

I held on to him like he was the last lifeboat on the sinking *Titanic*. Teek was not one for emotional moments so he just lay there like a dead plant. He didn't say a word nor did he offer an embrace in exchange for mine. I was convinced that this time I had really done it. He hated me, and this much I knew. It was over. Done. Finished. The end. I mourned the loss for a beat, but only till he succumbed and reached out his arms and held me back. And then I felt whole, but only for the moment.

And over the next several days . . .

I apologized.

I begged.

I pleaded.

I bought him things, expensive things.

I played all eighteen holes on the world's largest course of kiss-your-ass. I did whatever I could to make it right with him.

Why?

The same reason I always did: I needed him more than he needed me.

Thank God this kind of devastation wasn't a daily production. Teek only got hurt when I needed to hurt him. But the sad thing was I needed to hurt him a lot. It was difficult to explain this to Teek. He just didn't get it. It was hard for him to understand that his pain was an integral part of my pleasure. His pain got me off in a way that I needed to get off. When I saw him bleed or suffer, I felt in control. When he was in his greatest agony, it was then I felt most liberated. When he was down on all fours trying to regroup from an unsuspected blow to the groin or a painful twist of his balls, it was orgasmic for me. And again, Teek just couldn't understand.

Sex was as frightening as it was erotic. And if there was one thing Teek had going for him, he was smooth with his parts, but his man-parts were large, almost too large. That's what frightened me most. But when it got too serious, Teek knew. He was like a tuned animal, easily capable of sensing unvoiced fear. And when he felt it, he'd back off. His steel erection would go limp on cue if he thought it too much for me. He had commanding control and even at the threshold of orgasm, if I got scared, he would stop. He was elegant, strong, wise, and bold enough to guide me to safety's harbor in the uncharted waters of our convoluted sex games. Even rough, he was gentle. In total obscurity, his body dialed in to my channel and tuned to my vibe. And now he was inside of me, moving so freely, uninhibited by the laws of nature.

With each push I fell farther into the mirror. He was dishing it good and I was riding like this was the last known penis in the Western hemisphere. But I wanted the sex over and the man dead. As I stared into Teek's eyes, I wanted him gone. *No, not him. Not him.* With each vigorous thrust throwing me deeper into my own reflection, I wanted to rip him from his flesh with my hands. *But no, not him. Not him.*

"Yes," I moaned. "Yes."

I could see his demise, a pathetic and invasive life crushed from its life source.

I was the master and he the slave.

I was the ruler and he my subject.

I held the power . . .

And I was starting to believe the fantasy until . . .

"Oh shit!" Teek interrupted.

"What?" I asked, my moan against his.

"I'm . . ." He didn't finish.

Didn't have to.

Coming. I'm coming.
The room spilled to nothing.

The good feeling I was riding died a sudden death. The high dropped to a low and I plummeted into depression. I always did afterwards. I could never hold on to the *emotion* longer than the act itself. And God only knew from what wishing-well my post-orgasmic response would be drawn, and what it would deliver upon its arrival.

My body stopped moving and his nearly collapsed against me. He pulled out limp, and satisfied perhaps.

I sat back, apathetic, as I reached into his pants and pulled out a cigarette.

As I lit the cigarette and took a drag off it, I looked through the door's crack, only to see Ridge Huston just beyond the door, watching, masturbating.

His feet were planted on the ground. In a quick glance I was able to ascertain that he had been there awhile. His eyes were glazed, his pupils dilated.

I made firm, hard eye contact with Huston before slamming the door shut with the heel of my bare foot.

"Prick," I mumbled to myself.

"What?" said Teek, turning toward the door as he grabbed the cigarette out of my mouth.

"Huston," I said.

Teek did a double-take.

"Huston?" he asked.

"He was watching," I said without emotion.

Teek choked.

"He was watching?" he mimicked, with detectable panic in his voice. One could say he looked horrified. Perhaps horrified was normal and it was me, the abnormal one, who had little to no reaction. Well, actually, that wasn't true. I had responded all of my life and that's how I found myself on emotional overload, incapable of reacting anymore. I casually bent down and picked up the cigarette that had fallen out of Teek's mouth and onto the floor.

"Yes," I said, finally answering his question.

"He saw me . . . ?"

"Yes."

"He saw you . . . ?"

"Yes."

"He *saw* us!" he said, climbing a ladder to hysteria.

"Yes, I told you he was watching," I said, blowing past him. Teek's color drained and he turned pale.

"This may be a really dumb question but—*why?* Why was he watching?"

"What do you want me to say?" I snapped.

"Why was he watching, Symone?" he asked again, urgently.

"He was masturbating," I replied in a low voice.

"What the hell kind of family is this?" Teek asked himself, wiping the sweat from his brow.

"The kind you don't want to know," I said as I took Madeline's fine linen, wet it, and wiped Teek's sperm from my legs. "We forgot . . . ," I said.

"Forgot what?" he asked.

"To use a condom," I said matter-of-factly.

"I have a bigger issue right now, Symone—"

"We can't forget anymore," I said, staring at my reflection in the mirror.

Teek shook his head. "Excuse me for interrupting the Planned Parenthood procession, but your father just stood here and watched us have sex in his bathroom"—said Teek, exasperated— "while he *masturbated?*"

"Don't worry," I said.

" 'Don't worry'?" he repeated.

"He's not my *real* father."

"Well, that makes me feel a whole lot better," Teek said sarcastically.

"I don't know what you want me to say," I said with little emotion.

"How about good night?" Teek replied sharply. "I know you're not expecting me to go back in there, sit down, and eat a meal with the man who just stood here and watched me have sex with his daughter," he said.

I threw the wet washcloth at Teek. "I told you he's not my real father, and that is *exactly* what I expect you to do."

"This is some weird shit, Symone."

"Please," I begged wearily.

"Come on! Think about what you're saying. How can I look this wacko in the eye?"

"Just do it," I said with finality and frayed nerves. "Now, turn the page and get off the topic."

I pulled up my underwear in silence as Teek got himself together.

"This is some freaky shit," I heard him mumbling.

I didn't respond.

"Some real freaky shit"—as if he needed to say it twice. "What am I supposed to do," he insisted, "shake his hand and say, 'Thank you, sir. Thank you for your wife's fine turkey and your daughter's tasty pussy'?"

I couldn't bear it anymore. Before I could compose myself I hauled off and slapped him. I couldn't tolerate any more whining, complaining. I couldn't believe what a big deal he was making out of the whole thing.

But maybe it *was* a big deal. Maybe I was just numb.

Perhaps I was already dead and not privy to the fact that I

was gone. I mean, really. Why didn't it phase me that Huston could entertain himself by watching me perform while masturbating to my every twist, my every turn? Why didn't that strike me as odd? I knew it wasn't normal. But was it *that* absurd?

"Are you out of your mind, Symone?" Teek howled, grabbing his stinging cheek, bringing me back to reality by his harsh tone.

"Baby—" I reached for him.

He pulled away. "I'm done!" he said, throwing up his hands.

When those words rolled off his tongue I went straight into a panic. What was he really saying?

I'm leaving you.

Gone.

You're all alone.

You'll die alone with no one to hold your hand.

I nearly buckled.

"Are you man enough for me to hit you back?" he demanded with high aggravation. Teek had never laid a hand on me but I wasn't sure that wasn't about to change.

"I'm sorry," I apologized. "I just couldn't take it anymore, Teek. The whining—"

" 'Whining'!" he yelled.

"No, no, not whining," I corrected myself.

I was shaken. At that moment I was about to abandon dignity, drop to my knees, and beg.

I may have talked a big game, but when shit came to shinola, Teek had the upper hand because he *could* walk out of my life. Walking was not an option for me. Especially with Natalie gone now, I felt so vulnerable. In love, the one who loves less will always be freer.

"I'm out of here, Symone."

"Where are you going?" I asked, trying not to sound so desperate.

He didn't answer.

"Teek?"

"I don't know," he said. If he was going home, I could breathe because I would see him again. If he was going somewhere else, it meant he wouldn't be back. It also meant I would never see him again. It meant good-bye.

So I played my last hand.

"Huston raped me," I said softly.

And much like I expected, the earth stood still. Teek was devastated, speechless, and there was nothing but silence for a long, long time. I had hoped for a better way to break the news but a better way never arrived. Well, so much for a proper explanation.

"Oh, baby," said Teek. "Oh, baby . . . ," he said, pulling me to him. "When did this happen?" he asked.

"When didn't it happen?" I asked.

His eyes watered.

"More than once?" he asked softly.

I simply looked away. Who could bear to count?

Of course I knew it had been 326 times over a four-and-a-half-year period, but I would take that number with me to the grave.

"And there's more," I added, frustrated. "He bought out Sammy's partnership in the gallery. So he's my new partner now."

Teek stood there, dumbfounded and overwhelmed. It was just too awkward to talk about it all so I let us both off the hook by suggesting, "We should go back now."

Hollowed by the news, Teek didn't put up a fuss. He just nodded. And as I opened the bathroom door, he grabbed me and pulled me to him and held me tight. He wrapped his body around me with earnest regret for the years of neglected pain.

He held me with such compassion, desperate to share my hurt, or at least lift some of it from my being. But his arms would never be big enough, nor his back strong enough to carry this load.

"Let's get out of here, Symone. Let's leave right now and never look back. You don't need these people," he said.

"But I do need my gallery and I'm going to get it back," I said with conviction and a little desperation. "I can't walk now, Teek, I just can't, not with the gallery at stake."

I looked into his big, oddly colored eyes and knew that for the first time he *understood*. He nodded in agreement and together we stood in silence, completely connected.

CHAPTER FIFTEEN

"Nice of you to join us," Madeline said sarcastically as she gestured to our seats.

"Sit," she demanded.

And we did.

By this time Huston had seated himself at the head of the table. He was almost boastful in his stance, gloating in a subtle but predictable manner.

Teek was silent and awkwardly uncomfortable now. And I, so accustomed to playing the role of the stoic, felt vaguely unaffected by it all. But I was affected. *So* affected.

"Symone, did your gentleman friend meet Mr. Huston?" Madeline asked.

"Unfortunately," I said without hesitation as I struggled to pull my chair closer to the table.

Huston looked at me, but then again, he always looked at me. He never troubled himself to respond to my wisecracks and digs beneath the surface. He was above it all, so to speak. But I use that term loosely because you and I know that Huston was above nothing. It wasn't his style. Huston didn't use words because he had something more powerful. *Actions.* And when he was good and ready he'd pull out the rug, gouge the jugular, and stand in front of the sun to hinder the light from passing through. Guaranteed. But his immediate attention was turned toward Teek.

"What's your name, son?" asked Huston.

Huston addressed Teek by the word "son" because he knew I loathed the word.

"It ain't '*son*,'" I shot back.

"Teek," said my beautiful man.

"A pleasure," Huston said, extending his hand from across the table. But Teek didn't immediately accept. His pause was indication that he knew. *I never should have told him. Then he wouldn't be accountable for the knowledge and this wouldn't be as awkward a moment as it was turning out to be.*

No one moved and we were all horrified that the truth was going to push its ugly, splintered head from beneath the big black rock. And that it would crawl out with bloodshot eyes and dying scales on its back, infectious sores leaking our history. And we couldn't afford that. No one, including me, was prepared to deal with the truth in its raw, cryptic form. In many ways it was easier to step around the big black rock than disturb it.

After a dangerously long pause, Teek finally accepted Huston's hand. The room was spinning on tension and I was scared it might blow. Not that everyone in the room didn't already know what had happened, but it probably would have been in poor taste to have asked Huston to pass the bread and offer an explanation of why he had raped me, all in the same breath.

But Teek didn't blow it. He kept his composure and restrained his tongue from commenting. He made sure the dirty truth stayed under the rock because it just wasn't time for it to be born yet. And this certainly would have qualified as a premature birth.

"What type of work do you do, son?" asked Huston.

"Construction," said Teek.

"Who are you working for?" asked Huston.

Huston didn't give a shit about Teek's employer. He was setting him up.

"City," said Teek.

"What project?" prodded Huston.

"It's seasonal," said Teek.

"Meaning?" Huston demanded.

"Let it go," I quickly replied to Huston. "Why are you so concerned?"

"I'm always concerned about my children and the company they keep," he said with shallow sincerity.

"I'm unemployed, sir," Teek said bitterly.

"Ouch! No income," Audrey injected sarcastically.

"Back off," I snapped, intercepting the heat.

"If you're embarrassed by your friends, perhaps you should associate with a better class of people, Symone," Huston said sharply, pulling the chain where the link was weak.

"Ridge," cautioned Madeline. She constructed a look on her face, which translated as, *Down, boy, down.* And without uttering a sound, she advised Huston against going in for the kill. And I concurred, demanding through eyes and expression that he let it go.

"However, I am not referring to this young man here at my

table. No, actually, I like this young man. I don't know you, son, but I like your style," Huston said excitedly. "Goddamn it, I like your style."

Teek turned to me as if to say, *Your turn to lead this dance.* He looked lost, and rightly so.

"And if you're interested," said Huston as he handed Teek a business card, "I'll help you start earning your keep in this world."

I stopped midchew.

There goes another rug, another puncture of the jugular. He didn't want to give my man a job any more than he wanted to become my partner in the gallery.

Don't you get it by now? Everything had an agenda. Subtext. Footnotes. Every move he made was subtitled, and if you were going to outsmart him or outlive him, then it was essential to learn the art of reading between the lines—his lines.

Huston wanted to get under my skin by getting to my man. And offering Teek employment was his way of making sure I knew that nothing would be mine unless he provided it to me. Not Teek, the gallery, nor my life really belonged to me as long as Huston was alive.

But it was just a matter of time before the whole production blew up. I mean, really, the truth wouldn't stay buried forever. Inevitably it would creep upward and outward—on the sunniest day of the year, no doubt. And even if it didn't, there's always one disgruntled character in every plot whose entire existence is focused upon flipping over the big black rock.

I glanced around the room and wondered again, *Why am I here?* I had to keep asking because I was never quite sure. And even when I was sure, I still didn't *know*.

I watched Audrey pick at Madeline's dry, exotic bird and suck up to Huston, trying to reclaim her inheritance. And though we had all been screwed by Huston—again—everyone pretended everything was okay. But that was the norm in our house. Nothing was okay until everything was not okay; then it was just fine.

There were no guests to hide behind this year, which meant no extra bodies to absorb my hate and rage. Every year on Thanksgiving Day, the Hustons always had a party and everyone would come. There was a mini–holiday gathering slated for later on tonight. It was part of Eden tradition, and the part I despised.

Huston had requested this year's Thanksgiving dinner be an intimate one with family, primarily because of the mandated meeting filled with legal mumbo jumbo. Meetings like this were unusual for a holiday but not so unusual for a bastard.

My spirit was raw and uneasy. I felt like I was at a wedding where the couple was going directly from the ceremony straight to divorce court.

I stared into the faces of those dining with me and saw my own reflection. I reached down to rub my numb leg and my fingers stung. Why? Perhaps because I was a walking, breathing, flammable *wound*.

I ached as I watched Chandler down her fourth helping of white-meat turkey. I could see through her lily-white skin, down to the raw, bleeding soul she was hiding under the asphyxiation of cellulite.

Why are you killing yourself? I wanted to ask, but felt too tired to echo the words. And then I remembered as if I had never forgot at all.

It was the first time I played in the snow.

I was almost thirteen. I had seen plenty of snow growing up in Dorchester, but before I could get my shoes on to step outside, the snow would form an alliance with mud and dirt and turn to sludge. It was an unfriendly combination of gunk. We called it "gunk" because it was gross and it stunk—*gunk*. When I moved to Eden Village I noticed: the better the zip code, the whiter the snow. Eden Village's snow was majestic.

It appeared that God had dropped a giant, white, fluffy blanket out of the sky and spread it over the pricey homes. It was beautiful, untouched, unblemished. There were no footprints or tire tracks. There was no trash, mud, or homeless men's urine staining God's white blanket. Indeed it was flawless.

It was about five o'clock in the morning and I had just been awakened by one of the many nightmares that by then I was experiencing on a daily basis. Too frightened to go back to sleep, I opened the French doors of my bedroom and wandered out onto the massive grounds of the estate.

I could literally see for miles beyond me.

So what did I do?

Closed my eyes.

I closed my eyes and took delight in the fact that the Earth was finally still. At long last it was still.

It was not moving. Not rushing. Not being rude or pushy. No one was bitching and moaning. No one was being assaulted or mugged, beaten, verbally abused, or violated.

I was so engaged by the moment that I suddenly felt the compulsive urge to run. To sprint. To leap. To dash. And to plummet through the air without fear of ever being grounded again.

And so I did.

In my thin nightgown I plowed down the hillside, jumping and falling. I picked myself up only to fall again. I tumbled, laughed, and rolled. I was freezing, sopping wet, and partially delirious. But I felt good. I felt damn good.

I glanced up at God and winked.

"I'm having a good day!" I screamed to God. "I'm having a really great day!"

Why not scream?

Who was going to hear me?

Who was there to wake at five in the morning in the middle of nowhere?

I continued to roll in the snow like a madwoman.

I was beyond control but loving every moment of my madness.

I rolled onto my back and stared at the sky.

I'm not dead after all.

I rolled again, but this time I noticed a splotch of blood in the snow where I had lain.

I sat up and stared at it, rubbing my fingers through it for confirmation.

Indeed it was red. Indeed it was blood.

I had only one question as the red turned to crimson on my fingertips: *It this about to dim my sunny day?*

I looked between my legs and saw blood through my underwear. *Again?* I thought. Mother Nature was knocking and I had to let her in.

Agitated, I stood up. I suddenly felt very heavy as I dragged my feet through the snow. I could also feel the edge of the wind as it ripped through my gown.

My skin bubbled with chill and my teeth instinctively chattered. My stained red fingers felt hollow and dense at the same time. My lips were so heavy I thought they would fall off and plant themselves in the snow for the winter.

I suddenly began to imagine returning to the house for breakfast with frozen hands that had webbed like a duck from the cold.

I would politely sit at the table without drawing attention to myself till I tried to speak. And then everyone would see.

Audrey would be the first to respond. She would squeal, *The bitch has no lips! The bitch has no lips!* And to my chagrin someone else would notice: *And her hands are webbed like a duck's!*

I would try to hide my hands by sitting on them, and conceal my lips by growing my nose longer.

I would look up and they would see that my eyes had frozen from winter's wrath and my eyeballs were like those of a vulture.

Now, wouldn't that be a sight?

And since we both knew I'd have no lips, I'd simply gesture for them to pass the mother-loving eggs.

I played this game of intellectual ping-pong, tossing ludicrous scenarios back and forth against my imagination. It was then I had to remind myself: *It's not that serious, Symone. It's just your period.*

It wasn't the end of civilization as we knew it; it was just that time of the month.

I didn't need a diplomatic explanation on foreign policy, nor did I need to calculate the square root of infinity. I just needed a super-maxi with winglike tips to catch the dribbles that rolled to the edge.

If I trudged my bloated body back to the house and found only tampons in the cabinet, I would probably flip out and kill everybody in the state of Michigan.

I panicked at the sight of tampons. I didn't know how to use them. I tried once, and what should have been a five-second insertion wound up taking two hours. One hour to shove the thing in and one hour of squatting on the floor with my nose up my butt looking for it.

I wanted to take out a contract on the bastard who slapped the misleading words "Easy Glide" on the box. There was nothing easy about gliding a spark plug up your vaginal tract.

Call me crazy, but I just felt awkward walking around with an oversized Q-tip shoved up my twat with a string on the end that I hoped wouldn't break so I could get the damn thing out.

With blood freely flowing and my mind wandering without supervised direction, I easily could have been categorized as a menace to society.

I continued back to the house, keeping up the madness of mentally challenging tampons against maxipads. And I could have entertained myself with this drama all day—really, I could. And I probably would have, had I not been distracted by dancing shadows in a window at the opposite end of the estate.

This particular area was secluded, purposely tucked away from the rest of the compound. So you will understand my fascination with its occupancy and signs of life.

I squinted, moving closer to the window. I desperately wanted to know what was going on in this off-limits area.

I closed in on the shadows to examine their contents. I flattened my nose into the cold glass and peered inside. Then I backed away in horror. It was not the subzero temperature that elicited such a response. It was Huston.

He was standing in the room with his hands pressed around Chandler's head. And though he stood with his back facing me I could see what was going on. His pants were lowered to his ankles and Chandler was performing oral sex on him. Through a gap in his legs I could see Chandler's dreadful expression and the stained, dry tears on her cheeks.

I could not believe it! I was so distraught by what I had just seen that I begged it to be an illusion. Astonishment left me weak and I collapsed into the snow.

My heart was beating so hard I thought it would definitely explode. I heard thunder sounds in my ears as I tried to calm the panic that was well on its way to ascension.

Could they, too, hear the beating drum in my heart?

Could they tune their ears to detect the depth of my breath?

Were they privy to the deafening screams inside my head?

Would I look up only to be greeted by horror on their faces?
I caught you.
Caught you red-handed.
Would Huston kill me if he knew that I knew what nobody wanted to know?

Terrified, I crawled away from the window.

Chandler was in trouble and Chandler was in pain. She was the victim, and I, the passerby and the one who got away, this time. While Chandler remained—to be stricken of all that made her whole, of all that made her real, and all that made her human. Would she ever be human again? Would I? Violated and dishonored and shamed into silence. Would we ever be human again?

I had been in pain. I, too, had been hurt, but I could not stop to save her. I could barely save myself. *Don't wait on me to rescue you, Chandler. After all, I'm the half-nutty bat still waiting on a six-foot-six fictional messiah named Abigail to come and rescue me. And she's so late on her deliverance that even her colony of deaf-mutes is mocking me. I cannot come to save you because I cannot save myself.*

I was scared and a coward. Yes, too mortified to do the right thing. Too constrained by one thought—*Coulda been my fault*—and maybe I deserved this. And if I deserved it, then maybe Chandler did, too. If we didn't deserve this atrocity, then why—*Tell me, God, and tell me, Abigail and your faithful followers of deaf-mutes*—why was this happening to *us*? And didn't *every* little girl grow up like this? With their daddy's dick not too far behind them, *inside* them? Didn't *every* girl grow up like this, playing house with dildos and ding-a-lings and every other shameful thing? Didn't we all grow up like this?

I felt guilty, but at the same time relieved. I wasn't relieved that this horrible thing was happening to Chandler; I was just grateful that it wasn't happening to me. And there went a crack in the wall of my rare and brittle existence.

I froze the frame and returned from wherever it was I had gone. These journeys, flashbacks, or memories—call them what you want—always dumped me out at the places I'd spent most of my life running away from.

As I drifted back to current events, I saw that everyone at the table was gone. Well, everyone except Teek and Huston. Teek sat beside me and Huston sat at the end like the king of a castle or the president of a nation. He was the greatest illusion the world would never know, and his true role in society was "*scum.*" He was a great body without a soul. A brilliant mind without a conscience. And when I added all the sums of his parts together, still they equaled nothing.

I stared at him without saying a word and I could feel Teek's hand on my knee, offering moral support.

Huston stared back, sipping wine slowly and on purpose, coercing me back to the first time he had raped me, right here in this very room.

I could cut his throat—really, I could. Slip the sharpest knife purposely over a primary artery and watch him bleed to death, capture his blood in a beautiful glass, and toast his departure.

"There are going to be some changes at the gallery," he said flatly.

"Is that so?" I challenged.

"Quite so," he quickly injected. "For starters, the artwork you purchase—"

"*What* about the art?"

"We're going to upgrade it. No more junk," he snapped, with sarcastic emphasis on the word "junk." And I felt myself burning. "That weird stuff you purchase."

"She loves what the art represents," said Teek, coming to my defense. But he was quieted following a penetrating look from the Beast.

"The artwork I purchase represents the human condition, but you probably don't know anything about the human condition because you would first have to be human to understand it," I retorted.

"That was the old business," he said, dismissing me.

"Bullshit," I objected.

"Be careful. The business is now under new management," he said under a low voice. He leaned toward me to press his point and I backed away to exert mine.

"Well, I can't stand the new management," I said, dragging out the words in a low, hollow voice. Teek shot a look at me, perhaps surprised by my candor.

"You can't afford to run this gallery without me. So don't cross me," Huston said in a calm and eerie manner.

"This is *my* gallery. It belongs to me, not you."

"On the contrary," he said. "It belongs to *us*, dear. It is as much mine now as it is yours. And do you know *why*, Symone? Because I paid to have that privilege."

"Money can't buy everything," was my only comment.

"No, but it can buy most things," Huston declared with a smirk on his face. "So your point is moot, as always," he said, gloating.

"Young man," Huston said now, to Teek, "have you toured the grounds yet?" he asked, changing gears.

Teek looked at me before responding as though it were a trick question. I didn't know—maybe it *was* a trick question—so I could offer no direction through the blank expression on my face.

"No," Teek replied cautiously.

"Then I say you come with me and I'll show you around this enchanting palace," Huston suggested. "What do you say, Symone?" he asked. "Does his leash extend that far? Can I show him around the grounds?" he pressed, with biting sarcasm, the epitome of a motherfucker.

I nodded, giving Teek consent, and he stood up with hesitation. I cut a look to Huston so sharp it could have burned a hole through his skin. His eyes locked with mine and he threw the glare right back and whispered into my ear, "What's mine is mine, and what's yours once again is mine. And if you challenge me, push me, or piss me off, I will punish you," he said, the fire of Satan rolling from his tongue.

Little girl blue, go blow your horn.
Huston just did you once again.

I clenched my fists together, almost grunting, using an internal force to hold me back—back from his groin and his throat and his heart. I could have killed him right there on the spot.

"We're together again, baby," Huston said quietly as he slid from the table, departing with Teek, leaving me there, cemented in the dirty memories of his dry semen and my hot tears.

I sat there.

Just sat there.

Couldn't move.

Like a dummy.

Like a puppet.

Like clay.

Like a mute.

Like death.

Like me.

Like *me*.

Waiting on someone to rescue me, again.

Waiting for someone to care about this little black white girl who was all grown up but still couldn't move with him inside of me. All over me, rocking and stroking me. His skin, my skin, intertwined like that. So wrong, so raw, so real in the dark. *Get off and stop turning me over for more.* This little black white girl turned dummy and puppet, returned to clay like a mute, like death, that's me. That girl over there—didn't you know that was *me?*

Shortly after Huston left, Chandler returned, only to find me sitting lifelessly in the chair, like a wooden doll in need of resuscitation.

"Are you there?" she asked in jest.

"I am . . . I think," I said to her.

I think I am, I said to myself.

She sat beside me and began to eat again. This was her fifth helping. No, could have been her sixth. I didn't know. Lost count at four.

"Where is everybody?" I asked.

"They're in the gallery looking at Mom's new pieces," she said, rolling her eyes. "She just had some stuff shipped in that she's all psyched about."

Madeline was an art enthusiast. The mansion housed its own three thousand–square–foot gallery full of priceless art. When she made new purchases, we were automatically expected to spend hours drooling over the work, even if we didn't like it. And I never liked it, any of it. I didn't like Madeline's taste and Madeline didn't like mine. She tolerated what I did for a living and I tolerated what she did for a life.

She had never even been to my gallery. There was always something to keep her away: charity luncheons, afternoon tea parties with the old bitches down at the bridge club, and midday retreats to Eden's day spa. I interpreted her behavior as a general lack of interest in anybody's world but her own. Madeline was drunk on the nectar of terminal self-involvement.

"Where is your boyfriend?" Chandler asked, referring to Teek.

"Touring with your father," I said with a frown.

"He's cute, Symone," she said, with a giant smile that screamed, *Schoolgirl crush.*

"Yeah, I think so, too . . ."

"Do you want to marry him?" she asked.

Good question. And one I did not how to answer so I settled for ambiguity. "I don't know."

Chandler quickly turned her attention away from the conversation and to the food. She lost interest in everything around her as she honed in on the plate like a foreign missile on radar. She pushed the mashed potatoes to the left, sweet potatoes to the right, and cranberries to the center, while she gathered another plate to sample sweets.

I watched in horror, thinking that one day I could become this, too. A brutal slave of caloric overload, doing hard time in a shell of obesity. The sight was violent and horrific enough to scare me straight into anorexia: *I'll never eat again*, I felt like saying, *never eat again.*

I didn't mean to stare but I did. I chastised myself, saying, *Symone, don't stare. Please don't stare. You'll only upset her.*

Everywhere Chandler went, people stared, dumbfounded by her mounds of flesh. And I didn't want to be one of those dazed onlookers whose thoughts could be deciphered by the expression on their face: *How did she get so big?*

"Entertained?" she asked, catching my eyes in the act.

"What?"

"Are you amused by watching me eat?" she asked angrily. The food was like a drug that brought out the ugly. Witnessing the change was enough to send me swirling into flashbacks of my days with Dolores.

"No," I said, looking away.

"Do you think I'm enjoying the food?" she asked.

"Maybe," I replied, not sure.

"You're wrong," she snapped. "The food is enjoying *me*." She took a giant spoonful of mashed potatoes, sucked them down, and swallowed hard. "Do you think I eat because I'm hungry?"

"No."

"Do you think I like being fat?"

"I think you like being safe," I replied without hesitating. "Maybe the food helps you feel safe—I don't know ... I'm not a therapist but I've slept with enough of them to heal the whole goddamn world," I said, somewhere between joking and being dead serious.

"I am fat, Symone. Haven't you noticed?" she asked, eyes tearing. "Cellulite is my fashion statement. I purchase yacht covers and use them for summer dresses."

She stared into space, disengaging from herself.

"I love being fat," she whispered sarcastically. "There's nothing like seeing the world through the eyes of a fat person. I am the greatest minority there is—fat *and* sad."

As Chandler spoke, her skin jiggled, almost as if her body were mocking her. Her eyes were watering so heavily, I knew it was just a matter of time before she broke.

"Chandler," I said sternly, "it's okay." I reached out, grabbed her arm, and held on. "The giraffes are smiling today. The giraffes are smiling all day long," I said. This appeared to be a nonsensical statement but it meant something to her. And who was I to judge? Hell, my messiah was the queen of a colony of deaf-mutes, remember?

"Okay," said Chandler.

Her eyes dried and the trembling ceased.

Chandler loved giraffes. Her bedroom was a mausoleum dedicated to the long-necked beast. She had pictures, jewelry, trinkets, linens, seat covers, and even her toilet seat had a giraffe on the top. She worshiped the animal. Don't ask how or why, but when the giraffes were smiling, she was calm.

I also had found the opposite to be true.

If you got your kicks by watching a grown, fat woman cry, all you had to do was tell her the giraffes were restless and she'd tear the place apart.

When we were children, Audrey thought it was cute to play head games with Chandler, not always being sensitive to Chandler's frail condition. Audrey lived up to the words *Kids can be cruel*, and oftentimes took potshots at Chandler. She laughed at Chandler's obsession with giraffes and declared Chandler a mental case. But one day Audrey realized she, too, had "issues" and then it wasn't so funny anymore.

I had always tried to protect Chandler from Audrey's unnecessary abuse. It was the least I could do since I was not able to save her from Huston.

Chandler was weak. I was weak, too, but I was stronger than she was; therefore I felt obligated to shield her from the hurt that seemed duty-bound to find her. And when and where I could, I absorbed the sting of her burn and the flame of her fire. But it wasn't always an honest interception.

The giraffes are smiling, Chandler.

The world is bright, Chandler.

It's okay, Chandler.

We're okay, Chandler.

But that wasn't the truth anymore. Not that it ever was. How could I have lied to her so easily? And, the bigger question: How much of my own self would I assassinate to save someone else?

I knew the truth, and the truth was that the giraffes *weren't* smiling. They weren't on vacation, nor were they sunbathing on a nude beach. The giraffes were locked up in a cage in the back and they were all undergoing intensive psychotherapy. Most were on Valium, and the severely disturbed ones endured shock therapy.

That's what I saw when I looked at the giraffes. And all the little white lies I had told over the past decade about the giraffes only added to the number of cracks in the walls of my brittle existence. No wonder the walls were about to topple.

I couldn't lie anymore to protect Chandler; neither could I do it to protect myself. It was time to deal a straight hand, so I scooted my chair close to Chandler. I got so close I could smell her breath as she exhaled.

"Chandler . . . ," I whispered.

"Yes?"

"The giraffes are all fucked up," I said softly.

Her eyes widened, looking crazed.

"Their carcasses are spread over a barren desert and their insides are rotten to the bone."

"Oh my," said Chandler, dumbfounded and overwhelmed. She started to rock back and forth uncontrollably.

"Chandler," I pleaded, "stay with me."

"Oh my, oh my," she repeated again and again.

"Chandler," I said sternly, "the giraffes are—"

"Dead?" she asked, tears flowing down her chubby cheeks.

I held her hand as I looked into her eyes. I saw terror on her face, dents in her soul, and the horror of the secrets she'd kept under her skirt for so many years.

Huston had really done a number on Chandler. I couldn't believe he had been walking around for so many years in a self-induced daze of denial, wanting to know: *What's wrong with Chandler? What's wrong with Chandler?*

So many times I'd wanted to scream, You *are what's wrong with Chandler!*

"The giraffes are dead," Chandler said now, crying harder. "Who killed them? *Who?*" she cried aloud, squeezing my hand. She leapt from her seat and fell to the floor, weeping. And weeping. And weeping. She looked so helpless, pitifully tormented.

It scared me, and when I could no longer stand it, I forced her up from the ground and back into her chair. "Chandler. The giraffes are free. Don't cry for them. They are free."

"Free," she said, mimicking my words. Her face lifted from distress to relief. "They are free," she said again.

"Isn't it time for us to be free?" I asked as we sat holding hands.

"Yes," she said with resolution.

"Don't we deserve a happy ending?" I asked, as my eyes shifted from floor to ceiling, back to the floor.

This was a dangerous conversation we were about to have. We never discussed it. Never. It was time to flip over a big black rock.

"I saw what he did to you," I whispered.

She gasped, then covered her mouth with her hands. "You know?"

I nodded.

"I can't talk about this," she said, turning away from me, but I returned her face with my hands.

"Please," I said, holding back the tears. "Please . . ."

"You have no idea what I've gone through—" she started to say, but I stopped her.

"Yes I do," I said softly.

She paused, then took a deep breath and let it go.

"He hurt me, too . . . ," I was barely able to say.

A long, draining silence clapped against walls that made no sound and then Chandler finally said her piece.

"When I was a little girl, I thought everybody's childhood ended early," she said. "Father came into my room, parted my legs, and climbed on top . . ." The words slowly hollowed into sobs.

I was horrified listening, imagining, and remembering. I watched her spill, losing much of herself in the process. There were so many layers of pain, shame, and guilt. How could one man be the cause of so much devastation?

In the name of all that was unholy, despicable, and grotesque, he owned them all. He had broken every rule and heart along the way. He had stolen, violated, tormented, and manipulated for no good reason other than the fact that he was evil. Now, *somebody* had to pay. Somebody should. And it couldn't always be us, the victims, who exacted the price with the blood of our own souls.

There had to be a justice that existed somewhere for the crimes committed against us. Surely there must be a universal scale grand enough to balance the whole thing out?

I just couldn't accept that this was *it*; that yesterday was over and I was expected to move on without so much as flinching from my past. Was I simply to ignore the "little things"? Little things like falling apart? Piece by piece by piece? Perhaps I should have dismantled myself and saved the world the trouble of witnessing my demise.

I had always contemplated the killing of a child molester, but on this unusual day the thoughts began to take on a different form, a realistic shape.

Huston didn't deserve to live another day. I wasn't God, but

I wasn't wrong, either, for making that decision. The thoughts turned solid and began to take on form and shape.

Chandler and I both shifted our eyes toward the floor, leaving them there as we spoke.

"Do you want to be *free*, Chandler?" I asked.

"Even more than I want to be thin," she said with conviction.

We were speechless as our eyes slowly rose from the dust.

And all the madness stopped . . .

CHAPTER SIXTEEN

The walk through the winding corridor that connected the east wing to the west left us with fading light. The passage was about a hundred feet in length but it felt infinite. The sun was getting sleepy and the moon was struggling to make an entrance.

Where had the time gone? Daylight had slipped through my fingers and was pouring itself out at the end of a long, hard day.

What were the others doing back at Madeline's gallery? Was her guided tour excruciatingly painful, or had she actually bought something worth looking at this time? And what about Teek? What was Huston filling his head with, on their misguided tour of "the palace"? What in God's name had Teek gotten himself into by agreeing to come home with me for the holidays? Didn't he know that by the time the turkey was cut, eaten, and expelled, that I would be well on my way to tilting . . . ?

As I stared down the long avenue of lean walls, the inevitable darkness became my only immediate concern.

We were losing light so rapidly I feared it was just a matter of time before I succumbed to a breakdown. I pressed my hands desperately against the passageway, relying on sturdy walls to hold me up. Chandler and I were students of the blind, shuffling one foot in front of the other, unaware of what lay just ahead.

Her feet were much heavier than mine, and mine already had started to feel like two lead plates. So I can just imagine how heavy her feet must have felt.

The sputter of her feet as she pulled them up from behind her colossal frame was starting to overtake me. The gushing sound of dragging flesh danced against the most sensitive part of my nerves.

"Pick up your feet," I growled.

I'm trying," she said. Her breathing was labored and her body weak.

As we continued, Chandler's wheezing progressed. She could have had an asthma attack right there in the middle of the hallway and I didn't even have her inhaler.

"Wait . . . ," she puffed. "I need to take a break."

"We're on a mission, Chandler. We don't have time for a break," I snapped.

"I can't breathe," she said with tears in her eyes.

Dang.

Dang.

Dang.

I felt sorry for her, but at this point compassion would only be a hindrance.

"How long?" I asked, trying to be calm. I didn't want to frighten her with my growing agitation.

"Five minutes," she said, wilting to the floor. Her once-peachy complexion was turning close to blue.

"Okay. You sit here and rest. I'll keep going," I said with firm conviction.

Chandler breathed a sigh of relief. She seemed content, but I didn't know why. She had aborted the mission before the job was complete. And even though she had said it would just be a five-minute break, I knew it was over for Chandler. She would soon succumb to aches, pains, and out-of-synch joints. This would be followed by a dissertation on hemorrhoids and constipation.

I had to go on without her. How else was I going to get down the hallway to the gallery where Huston kept his guns? And if I didn't get the gun then I couldn't shoot him. And if I couldn't shoot him, he'd never die. And not only would he not die, but he'd live to see another day. Not just another day, but another day of my pain.

"Are you sure about that?" asked Chandler. "The hallway is pretty dark."

"I know the hallway is dark!" I said, almost coming unglued.

"Don't take it out on me because you're scared of the dark!" said Chandler.

Chandler was right. I couldn't be angry with her because I was a chickenshit. And being "*scared* of the dark" was an understatement—I was horrified.

The corridor was airy, light, and natural, but only in the day. At night the corridor was dark, illuminated by tiny floor lights. It was supposed to capture the essence of nighttime under the stars. But I never got the effect; it never made sense to me at all.

I clung to the walls so hard, my fingers bled at the nails. My legs felt suspended but at the same time weighted.

The air was cold. Still.

I felt the uncomfortable brush of invisible people rubbing against me without permission. I began to feel violated. But my immediate concern was *air*. Why was the air disappearing, slowly collapsing to the floor?

I lowered myself in desperate search of pockets of air, but there were no takers.

My vision was dimming and oxygen slipped through my flesh without filling my lungs.

How could this be?

I continued down the corridor, half bent to the ground. I was chilled but leaking perspiration in the same breath.

Deep inside I was hoping the end of the hallway would just blow up. If it blew I would have a justifiable excuse for not making it to the end. As it stood, the only excuse I had was that I was a pansy, a gutless coward. I didn't want to turn around and go back to Chandler without the gun.

I wanted a gun. I needed a gun. A gun was a means to the end. It was liberating. I couldn't wait to watch the glorious sight of Huston as he lay on the floor gagging on his last breath. The sheer pleasure of watching him die was reason enough to continue down the dimming, narrowing corridor.

But it was getting harder. The air was getting thinner. The place was colder. Darker. Lonelier.

The walls were not very gracious. They tried to cut me off, block me, squeeze me to death. They were purposefully trying to stop me . . . Why?

By this time the only way to breathe was to pant. And the only way to move was rapidly, precisely. Adrenaline surged through my body. The sweat had now begun to pour. My body stiffened and the hair on my neck stood erect.

"Oh, God," I cried aloud as I buckled to my knees.

The hallway was horribly dark.

Terrifyingly narrow.

Dreadfully long.

Painfully isolated.

I wasn't ready to die yet but I suddenly felt terribly close to the grave.

When I closed my eyes I saw myself lying in a casket wearing a beautiful lace dress. The dress was slit down the back to fit nicely over my stiff corpse. My hair was dry and jacked. My makeup was stale and layered to cover how horrible I looked from being dead.

"Oh, Jesus," I cried louder.

Why couldn't I go on? I was lying on the floor in the dark, paralyzed by my fear and helplessness.

It seemed like such an easy thing to do, walking a dimly lit hallway. But there was nothing easy about it.

I hated myself.

I was a failure.

Another day spent as a loser.

I was saddened to acknowledge that this would be one more thing I would have to add to my growing list of impossibilities.

A single tear streaked my cheek as I followed with hollow eyes the tracks I could not walk. I stared at the barren walkway devoid of my steps.

I would have to drag my ass back down the hallway to Chandler. She was too large to walk the hall and I was too scared. And which was worse?

She was trapped inside a fat person, and I, inside a frightened one. She was held captive by her physical body, and me, by my soul.

"Mission aborted," I said aloud.

I stood up, put my tail between my legs, and turned my back on the dark hallway. And suddenly . . . breathing was so much easier.

CHAPTER SEVENTEEN

"What happened?" Chandler asked, as if she didn't already know.

"I couldn't do it," I said coldly.

There was no need to elaborate because Chandler understood. All who knew me well, knew that darkness was my enemy.

"What do we do now?" she asked.

Why did I always have to find the answers in my trick bag? Didn't anybody else keep secrets up their sleeve?

"We wait," I said sternly. In other words, I didn't know what the hell we were going to do. And with that conclusion, we only had one option left: Audrey.

We found her standing shoulder-to-glass against a full-length mirror in one of the spare bedrooms. Her eyes dropped the length of her body while she stole moments to seduce her reflection.

She admired her glistening hair and whorish outfit. She massaged her delicate nose, ran her fingers teasingly over her brow. She fondled her breasts, applauding their perkiness and rubbed a quick hand over her backside.

I waited for Audrey to finish. And when the production looked about over it was time for the real show to begin.

"Audrey?" I called, startling her. She quivered a bit.

"What?" she asked.

"I need to talk to you."

"About?" she inquired, raising one brow imperialistically.

"I need your help."

She started to laugh and it echoed like the deafening sounds of church bells with a high-pitched shrill strong enough to cut flesh and bone. Her laughter was mocking, insulting.

I wanted to sock her, lay her out like a Louisiana pancake, but I didn't. Instead I chained my temper and held on. Petitioning Audrey meant I had pushed past desperate.

"What could you possibly want from me?" she asked, swinging and swaying from all the alcohol she had consumed.

"I need you to go to the gallery where Huston keeps his guns. Through the corridor."

"And?"

"I need a gun."

I was almost afraid to suggest that Audrey bring it back because she was so drunk she might blow her own head off by mistake.

"Gun? For what?" she asked, stumbling around the room, still grooming herself in the mirror.

"It's time," I said.

"For what?"

"Payback," I said after a long pause.

"Payback?" she repeated, after a longer one.

Her brow raised and she sobered. The buzz, the high, the lift, whatever she was on, was gone. It was gone because she *understood.*

"Oh, you're out of your mind!" she hissed.

"No," said Chandler from the other side of the room. "She's not crazy. We need your help, Audrey."

"You're in on this, too, Chandler?" asked Audrey, surprised. "I don't want anything to do with this. Count me out," she said, shaking her head while nervously lighting a cigarette.

"He hurt you bad one night," I said, exposing the raw nerve. "The night he tore you down there. I heard you through the door where I was standing just outside. I remember you begging him to stop because you could feel the tear."

Audrey froze.

So did Chandler.

The room was still for several minutes.

No one moved.

No one said a word and I don't even think anyone's heart was beating. We were suspended in time, crystallized by horror as we all ventured back to the most painful parts of our childhoods.

Audrey's breathing deepened, becoming more labored. She closed her eyes and put her hands over her ears, trying to shut down the nightmare.

"I remember," I said in a low voice.

Audrey refused to respond, just kept hiding behind denial.

"Audrey," I called to her.

"Audrey," Chandler followed.

And finally she spoke. "I can't stand the sight of Vaseline," she said, eyes filled with water.

"With Vaseline it was easier . . . ," she said as soft tears trickled down her face.

Chandler burst into tears and wept like a child. And I did as I had always done, played the part of the stoic. It was the only form of preservation I knew.

"He would come into my room reciting nursery rhymes," Audrey continued. " 'Hickory dickory dock . . . ',"

" 'Daddy just lost his clock . . . '," Chandler injected weakly.

" 'Hickory dickory blue . . . '," Audrey continued.

" 'His clock's *inside* of you . . . '," I finished.

"I was a little girl," said Audrey. "I couldn't fight him," she said.

"Couldn't win," said Chandler. "He had all of the power."

"*We* had all the pain," I concluded.

We could finish each other's sentences because we had lived the same experience and shared the same losses.

Audrey paused to regroup, then continued. "June thirteenth. It was really hot outside that day. Everyone was gone. And he came to me in the middle of the day and said it was time for nursery rhymes—that was the first time he actually penetrated me . . . I'll never forget that *feeling*. . . ."

"Of him being inside," said Chandler.

"And you just couldn't move," I said.

"Or breathe," said Audrey.

"Why did we stay?" I asked them.

"Where were we going to go?" asked Audrey.

"And who was going to believe us?" inserted Chandler.

I could feel Huston for days long after he had left my bedroom. I could smell the stench of his body and feel the glide of his skin. I remember the burn on my cheek from his unshaven face. And his sloppy, wet kisses that stained my body for good.

The three of us stood like ghosts in a gloom. Chandler was backed against the wall with her head hung low. Life always had Chandler backed against the wall.

Audrey stood center stage where she was probably most comfortable. Audrey always stood center stage, waiting for the big
bright light to be turned on. But today I doubt she would have
welcomed its glare.

And I stood close to a beautiful picture window, my eyes
focused on the other side. I was always looking to the other side,
dangling too close to the edge. And one day I would jump. I
would jump to be free or jump to die . . . whichever.

"I never told a soul," said Audrey in a haunting voice.

"Neither did I," said Chandler.

They both looked at me. And I turned away.

"So what do we do about it?" I asked them. "Do we spend
the rest of our lives crying ourselves to sleep at night?"

"We go to therapy," said Audrey.

"Been there. Done that," I quickly responded.

"There are support groups," said Chandler.

"Yeah," said Audrey. "We could get help."

"But that won't fix it," I snapped.

"Nothing's going to fix it," Chandler said, resonating defeat.
"We'll be broken the rest of our lives."

"Do you know what perfect justice is?" I asked them, but
neither answered. "Perfect justice is an eye for an eye."

"Meaning?"

"He took something from us that we can never get back," I
said. "So in return, we take something from him of equal value,
something that he can never get back . . ."

"His life," Chandler said quietly.

"Perfect justice," I said.

"It's wrong," said Audrey.

"Raping us was wrong," said Chandler.

"It's over!" screamed Audrey. "It's dead."

I grabbed Audrey's face between my hands and forced her to look in the mirror.

"Is it?" I asked.

She didn't answer.

I asked again.

"Is it over?"

Silence.

"When something dies it doesn't hurt anymore," said Chandler. "Aren't you still hurting, Audrey?"

CHAPTER EIGHTEEN

The three of us barreled down the dim hallway so fast that sparks danced on our heels. We walked side by side, swaying against one another as we slightly brushed hands on, hands off. To those who didn't know us, it would appear we were flirting. But we knew better what to call it—the dance of death.

I didn't mind Audrey's large breasts jumping into my space or Chandler's massive thighs crowding me. The inconvenience was temporary, or better yet, a trade. I tolerated them because they were going to help me kill Huston. Their strength would also help me get down this hallway.

The aggressive look on our faces confirmed we were not aborting the mission. Huston was as good as dead. *Somebody better call and order flowers for the funeral.*

This time, Chandler was doing well to keep beat with our

steps. I thought she would have been on a respirator by now, but she wasn't.

We walked in silence.

The mood was sobering.

Chandler's wheezing and coughing were growing louder and more unavoidable. Her varicose veins were bulging and hurting. The extra pounds were weighing heavily on her frame, tiring her out. And up until the point that the pain actually began to show on her face, I thought she might make it. But once the real pain set in, her journey was done. She sought relief in a nearby corner.

Audrey and I continued. There was no need for all of us to surrender at once. As we neared the darkest part of the hallway and just before it opened into the broad gallery, anxiety slammed against me like an unwelcome brick wall.

"Shit!" I screamed aloud, stopping in my tracks. I turned back to face the way we had come. "I can't make it, Audrey."

"Try," she said with pleading eyes.

"I can't."

"Turn around," Audrey begged.

I did as she commanded, turning to confront the corridor. It wasn't *that* long. It was just a walkway. Empty space. It was an instrument used to narrow the gap between this end and that end. No big deal. Right?

"Look how far you've come!" Audrey said.

"But look how far I've got to go," I said with a depleted stare as my eyes searched the balance of the distance.

It was then I knew I wouldn't make it. I just couldn't do it.

"Is the glass half empty or the glass half full?" asked Audrey, catering to psychobabble, a side effect of a lifetime of psychologists telling her how to think and what to feel.

"The glass fell off the counter years ago and broke into a

thousand pieces," I responded. "And don't you know I'm still walking around with the slivers in my heels?"

And with that I retreated.

Audrey turned around and continued the journey.

I stood stiff at first, then weak as a baby as my knees buckled. And I sobbed. I was so angry that I slammed my fist into the wall. And before I knew what had happened, everything went black.

I awoke to a single gunshot. It was a thunderous blast that blew beyond my ear. Had Audrey found the gun and shot herself by mistake? Was she lying on the floor bleeding to death? Was she waiting for me to rush to her side like a well-trained horse and whisk her away from danger? Was the story supposed to end like this?

"What was that?" I screamed to Chandler, who had crawled to where I stood. The sound of my squeaking, panicked voice frightened her.

"What? What!" she screamed. Her face was colorless and her breathing heavy, too heavy. "Symone, what's going on?"

"Gunshots!" I yelled.

"What?" Chandler asked, puzzled.

"Didn't you hear it?"

As the words left me I turned, to face the barrel of a gun.

"What's wrong?" asked Audrey, holding the gun. Chandler's eyes cut to mine.

"Nothing," said Chandler.

"Nothing," I agreed, especially after I saw that not only had the gun *not* been discharged, but it also had a silencer. It was then I knew the only gunshots I had heard were the ones in my head. Further confirmation that I was slipping, tilting.

Moments later we were huddled in a corner, sketching our brilliant scheme on paper with Audrey's eyeliner.

"We enter here," I said, drawing a mockup of the dining area. "We blow in like the SWAT team and take him down with a piece of lead right between the eyes . . ."

Chandler balked. "Sounds barbaric."

"Okay, you map out a more elegant way to kill him," I said, throwing my hands up.

"You don't have to get bent on the ends, Symone," Audrey said. "It wouldn't hurt if we tried to figure out a more humane way to do this. Just because it's murder doesn't mean we have to behave like animals."

"I agree with Audrey," Chandler said.

"This isn't euthanasia, it's an execution! There's no *polite* way to execute someone!"

"Symone, the plan is no good," Audrey said.

"No good," Chandler mimicked.

"You have to look at this logically," said Audrey. "And there are a lot of loose ends to your scenario."

"Like?" I challenged.

"The other guests, for one."

"There's Mom," Chandler mentioned.

"There's hired staff for this evening's event," Audrey continued.

"There's Dad's attorney," said Chandler. "And *your* boyfriend."

"What about these people? Do you kill them, too?" asked Audrey. "Do we kill everybody in the room just because they're here?"

As much as I hated to hear what they were saying, I knew they were correct. But I had chosen to play devil's advocate in favor of instant gratification. I wanted him dead now, and to be forced to settle for *later* was unacceptable under my terms. To hell with a good and reasonable plan, and if by chance others died in the process, I would regrettably call them "casualties." I would be sorry for the loss of innocent lives but I had also learned from my days in Dorchester that innocent people die every day.

This is where the line was drawn and I found myself struggling between Huston's inhumanity and my own. Treat a child like an animal and perhaps one day you shall have a monster on your hands.

"Symone?" Audrey called, bringing me back, awaiting direction.

"Yeah," I said.

"It's not going to work," said Audrey.

"Okay," I said. "We go back to the drawing board and replot the scenario," I said, sounding like a drill sergeant.

Audrey and Chandler both frowned. I could tell they were wilting.

"I guess we could do that," Audrey said, faint of heart. "Unless . . ."

"Unless what?" I asked, hanging on every word.

". . . Unless we opted for therapy instead," she said after a great pause.

"Yeah," mumbled Chandler in agreement with Audrey.

I lowered my head.

"Death is so permanent," whispered Chandler.

"Yeah, it is a long time, isn't it?" asked Audrey, in a slight daze.

Their zeal for vengeance had withered like a perishing flower unable to fulfill its obligation to bloom.

"Maybe we could try another day," said Audrey, trying not to disappoint me entirely.

"Another day might be better," Chandler quickly inserted.

"There's always tomorrow, Symone," Audrey concluded. "And tomorrow might be better."

But that wasn't true. Tomorrow would be worse than today and the day after that would be unbearable.

For them.

For us.

For me.

But for now I let them go. I no longer expected them to help dispose of Huston. How could I have ever pleaded for their aid in the assassination of someone they knew as their father? They were in fact after all *real* Hustons, and I . . . a shallow impostor who had taken on the name only as a result of the untimely passing of a heroin addict.

I wasn't a cold-blooded killer, though I was having trouble locating a conscience that now seemed lost forever. I was battling my demons and fighting so hard to stay human. Confused and brittle, I skirted around morality and outright insanity.

I knew Audrey and Chandler were right, much more "right" than I would ever be. But it now seemed too late to implement a backup plan, when the only plan I had was to kill the motherfucker.

It was out my hands, beyond reconsideration. The wheels had been set in motion and the plan was going down. It had taken on a life of its own and I felt more like a bystander than a perpetrator, swept away by atrocity, murder, guts, and more.

I would kill Ridge Huston, and this much I knew for sure. But I would protect Chandler and Audrey from the gore of the details. I would host an organized affair, and more than a thoughtless massacre or an ambush against the unsuspecting. He shouldn't die because I wanted him dead. He should die because dead was where he belonged. He had earned the grave he would soon lie in. And I could not wait to climax on his last breath. It would be the grandest orgasm I had ever known. This was a release I desperately *needed* to have, with mounting tension so intense I could barely contain it.

I would stand on top of the roof and wait until he escorted his final guest of the evening out onto the cobblestone drive. And when he least expected it, I would pull out a high-powered rifle with a scope and aim for the pitted part in the back of his head. I would hold my breath, count to three, and pull the trigger without a beat of hesitation.

And I would *come* as I watched the metal meet his flesh, ripping it to shreds. I would delight as I watched with great anticipation his hollow body crashing against the pavement, spilling the most intricate part of his brain matter out onto the stone. I would lick my lips in expectation of the details as I fixated on every drop of his O-positive blood as it flowed into the driveway. And I would *come* again—or not. Perhaps it would go down much differently. I didn't require a violent, bloody death to be satisfied. I wasn't crazy, just fed up, and any death would do.

But if he died too fast, I'd only have done him a favor by putting him out of his misery. And where would the glory be?

Huston's death was necessary for my rebirth. And beyond that there was no greater explanation for his timely demise.

Good night.

CHAPTER NINETEEN

It was just a matter of time.

And circumstance.

And opportunity.

And an alibi . . . and he would be dead.

It wasn't out of the question, nor was it implausible. This would be the Wonderland Alice never made it to and the ghetto part of Oz that Dorothy never saw.

I retreated into one of the guest bedrooms to regroup. I was beginning to feel "crazy." Nervous exhaustion had all but consumed me.

I sat down on the bed and stared at my reflection through the mirror. I wasn't a bad person, just a bitter one, losing everything from my self-esteem to a sane grip on the world around me.

How does one prepare for the killing of a child molester? I had killed before, so perhaps it would be easy.

I reflected back to the day and the place and the time. Soprano notes bounced off the walls, echoing brilliantly, cementing me to the bottom of the bloody leather pump I was holding.

By the time Madeline and Ridge reached the room it was over. And all they could do was look on in horror.

"Symone," gasped Madeline.

"She killed him!" screamed Audrey. "She killed him with the shoe!"

"Oh, God," said Madeline, turning away with her hands over her mouth.

"What in God's name did you do?" asked Huston, horrified.

"Froyman's gone," cried Audrey.

Madeline snatched Audrey into her arms and they quickly disappeared. And that left only me, Huston, and an ugly situation.

I had just turned fourteen. Audrey was twelve. And Froyman was dead. Froyman was a white bunny rabbit that Audrey received as a Christmas present from Madeline.

I was the suspect because I was holding the shoe. But it was an accident, a freakish one, no doubt. I had stepped on Froyman's head by mistake while trying on a pair of Madeline's spike heels.

But no one believed me.

Madeline coined me a "bloody-footed monster" and they tricked me into believing I was insane. And this was my first encounter with being "crazy."

CHAPTER TWENTY

Insane people seek out sane people to bring them back to sanity. And this was how Rosetta Lindquist entered the fourteenth year of my life. Not too long after the death of the rabbit, the Hustons feared I could have another "accident" so they sent me to a specialist. I had never met anyone like her. She was pretty, a notch away from beautiful in her appearance. She looked to be cut from the same cloth as me, part white, part black, half of everything and whole of nothing.

She was an unconventional, Harvard-trained shrink who had founded a place for nutty kids called the Bright Child Counseling Center. Craziest shit: tough love–meets–Disneyland. *Whatever.* Their mission statement: "We pull kids back from the dark and bring them back into the light." But as far as I could see, there wasn't a light bright enough nor an arm strong enough to snatch me from the cave I was hiding in.

I was forced to visit Rosetta once a week for counseling because I had started having problems. I was expelled from four different private schools for unacceptable behavior and I was also facing charges of arson for a fire that had been set across town. Of course, I never admitted to any of those trumped-up charges. Hey, if they wanted a perfect kid they should have been perfect parents. So I didn't feel guilty about my tenure as a delinquent.

During that time I felt as if my life were spiraling out of control. I was typically classified an intellectual preteen with a bad attitude and a predisposition to being a troublemaker.

I never intended on telling the entire story of my past because I didn't wish to be judged and labeled as unbalanced, but I was about as balanced as a kid who was being molested on a regular basis could be.

You could take me anywhere but you just couldn't take your eyes off me. I might rob you blind or jack up your cat. I didn't do these things on purpose. They were all accidental. I had reached a point in my life where I could no longer control myself and be accountable for my actions. But the very last thing I wanted to do was sit in a foreign place and "talk about it."

It was all a big hoax, the counseling. I was sent by the Beast to discover why it was I behaved like an animal. But the Beast already knew. If I told the truth, the Beast would cut off my head. But I had better tell her something because the Beast wanted answers. But I swear to God the bastard already knew.

I could tell her about Abigail the Messiah and that would satisfy her curiosity for the day, or at least for the hour. But Abigail was still mine and I was deliberate on my intention to withhold her from the public.

I resented sitting in front of Rosetta, who tried to decipher me like a complicated jigsaw puzzle. *No, no, baby,* I wanted to say, *these pieces don't fit.* But instead of speaking, I opted to close my eyes and disappear.

"What are you thinking about?" she asked, trying to penetrate me with her big black eyes.

"You don't really want to know," I said.

"I asked," she insisted.

"But you don't want to know."

"Why don't I?"

"It's not so nice," I said.

"How do you define 'nice'?"

"Not socially appropriate," I responded.

"And your definition of that?" she asked.

"Unacceptable," I barked.

"I'm impressed," she said.

"Why?" I asked.

"By the fact that you even concern yourself with what is and is not acceptable."

"I'm not concerned. I just don't want to offend you on our first visit."

"How would you define 'offensive'?"

"Listen, it's Rosetta, right? My IQ is 147. I can define any word you can pronounce. But we're not here for a spelling bee or a grammar session. So let's cut the bullshit," I said, flustered by it all.

"You're very direct for a fourteen-year-old," she said, holding her position. "Do you think what you just said offends me? Shocks me?"

She got up from her seat and began to circle me like an animal plotting to devour its prey. But she didn't intimidate me. She was much too beautiful to be intimidating with her creamy skin and long, eye-catching legs.

"All right, let's cut to the chase. I want to help you," she insisted. "What can I do to help you?"

I didn't bother to answer.

"What do you want?" she repeated sternly.

"I want you to go down on me," I said with a smirk on my face.

Smack!

Her hands slammed down on the desk with crippling force. And even though she scared me half to death, I barely flinched, but enough so that she saw.

"Good," she said, offering a smile.

This bitch must be psycho, I thought to myself.

" 'Good' what?" I asked, feeling my backside to make sure I hadn't peed all over myself.

"You scare," she said.

"I what?" I asked in disbelief.

"You were scared," she said casually while taking a seat back at her desk. She now seemed at ease and delighted with her progress.

"What are you talking about?" I asked her.

She paused a moment, probably trying to master her strategy before responding.

"I saw fear in your eyes," she replied.

"So? You scared me. Are you a legit shrink or one of those nutty professors?"

"If I can find fear I can find pain," she concluded.

"So?"

"And if I can find pain I can find a human being. I can find love and trust again," she said.

"And what's that going to do for me?" I asked sarcastically.

"Well, for starters perhaps you can reenter civilization and stop living on the island you've created for yourself."

"It ain't so bad on the island," I said, arched in my chair, appearing a lot cooler than I really was. "It ain't so bad at all."

"Aren't you lonely out there?" she asked.

"It's a trade-off," I barked.

"What do you mean?"

"I might be lonely but at least I'm safe."

She looked stumped.

"I want to give you a definition," I said.

"Of what?" her face brightened.

"Idealist," I said.

"Okay . . . ," she said, baffled.

" 'Idealist,' " I repeated. " 'An overeducated, Harvard-trained therapist who believes she'll earn her inflated fees by cracking my shell. Idealist,' " I said again.

"This concludes our session today," was all that she could say.

CHAPTER TWENTY-ONE

It wasn't over.

It rarely ever was.

The following week I returned to Rosetta again.

This time I sat in an oversized chair, slouching and smacking bubble gum to piss her off. I played with the puttylike goo, allowing it to dance on the rooftop of my mouth before plunging it beneath my tongue.

She sat in a bigger chair than I did, assaulting me with disapproval, or so I thought. The harder she stared the more I smacked the gum. The more I smacked, the harder she stared. We courted one another in this intimidating dance till it was obvious someone needed to break.

It was as if we were characters in a western. Two gunfighters involved in a bitter standoff. Both had to protect their reputation but neither was willing to die. But somebody always has to die. If they don't, the audience gets restless and asks for their money back. Or the townspeople get offended and kill both gunmen. It was the rule of the game. It was sportsmanship. It didn't make it right. As a matter of fact it very damn well could have been wrong, but that's just the way it was. And that's where we were.

I was hell-bent on holding my stance and so was she. I wanted to piss her off, make her feel worthless, low. Those weren't noble things to pursue, but I felt violated and therefore justified. She was trying to crack my shell, not intentionally, but if the price were right she would sell me down the river without a paddle or a boat. She never *said* that, but then again, she didn't have to. A lifetime of distrust had led me to the art of reading people before people read me.

I was very protective of the wall I had created. It was the only thing that separated me from the insane. Break my wall, steal my shell, and I'm just another name on some forgotten institution's list of active mental patients.

"Do you wonder if I'll ever speak to you?" I posed the question to break the silence.

"No," she said flatly.

"I *will* speak. But when I do I won't say anything."

"Suit yourself," she said.

"I think you're worried."

"Don't flatter yourself . . . ," she said.

"But isn't that your job?" I asked.

"I'm already emotionally healthy and I get paid whether you speak or not," she said.

"A girl after my own heart," I chuckled.

And after a long beat, she laughed, too. Laughter lifted the mood and broke down the tension. Not all of it, but some of it.

"You don't do this for the money," I finally said.

"You're right, I don't. And now that we've got *me* all figured out, let's do a little work on *you*."

"Do you know why you give a shit?" I pressed.

She threw up her hands.

"Because your self-esteem hangs in the balance with every one of your patients. Every shell you crack boosts your own ego. For every success, your overinflated esteem gives itself a high-five."

She raised her brow. "And for every failure?" she asked.

"Confirmation that we're all alone in this world and that no one saves anybody. The best we can do is stand around with our hands tied behind our backs while we watch the person next to us go down in the sand . . ."

"I'm not trying to save you, Symone," she said convincingly.

"But wouldn't it make you feel good if you could?"

Silence fell against the room like a heavy curtain closing on the final act. She wasn't there to save me, she was there to save herself. I never troubled myself to open up to Rosetta and unleash the demons. Turning over the big black rock in those days was never an option.

What would we do with the truth when it was out?

What will we do, oh, then?

On the morning the sun creeps up against the horizon covered in blood, dry semen, and toxicity, what would we do, oh, then?

I couldn't speak because I had no tongue, vocabulary, or rights. I was a weakling, a child. Socially dependent upon the structure of family for my survival. If I could have run away then I wouldn't be here now. I never found that hole in the sky to slip through, but God knows how I tried.

I never saw Rosetta again after that day. So much for mental-health therapy. She disappeared, or maybe it was I who disappeared, only to return to the castle in continuation of a courtship by the Beast.

Perhaps my life would have been easier to swallow if I could have moved beyond cringing during the act of my rape. I never said it would be better, just maybe a little easier.

CHAPTER TWENTY-TWO

I sat on the bed in one of the guest bedrooms and stared out the window. I wasn't looking for anything in particular, just me, if I could find her. Teek sat beside me, holding my hand and reading my heart.

"Baby, I'm worried about you," he said.

I lay back on the canopy bed, mesmerized by a draft as it rustled the delicate lace drapes that fell around the bed.

I took another moment to catch my focus and saw I was surrounded by elegant furniture that looked rather new. The room looked strange but felt familiar. There were pristine accessories carefully plotted and set in their place. Hollow and dense views converged in the room, offering multidimensional confusion. The room was low, then high. Tall, then short. It was almost human in its futile attempt to breathe and come to life on its own.

Outside the bedroom the sun had gone to sleep. The darkness had arrived—now how would I get out? Tomorrow would be too late to leave. I was prepared to exchange my Girl Scout outfit for that of a Green Beret.

Teek was naked, kneeling over me. He fumbled to unbutton my shirt because I kept on begging, "Make love to me, make love . . ."

I pulled on him, yanking and grabbing.

"Easy, baby," he advised. "Easy."

"I want you inside," I sputtered.

It seemed forever before his penis could get hard.

"You feel good, baby," he said, gently stroking my skin, more for his pleasure than my own.

"So do you," I said without touching him back. "So do you."

That was the last I remember of our conversation. I didn't really vanish but somehow I disappeared. And when I awoke I was covered in his blood.

CHAPTER TWENTY-THREE

My limbs shook while the rest of me stood still. Fine hair that ran down the course of my spine stood on end. I could feel my pulse beat on the sensitive side of my trim neckline.

Teek lay facedown on the bed with a bullet in the brain. The better part of the back of his head was missing. I was saturated in blood. I'd been in tough spots before, but this coined the infamous phrase, *My ass is in a jam.*

How was I going to explain this gorgeous man (who also happens to be one of my lovers) facedown in a pool of blood, presumably his own, dead because half of his brain is gone?

Imagine the pit that formed in my stomach when I looked up and saw slices of his brain matter splattered against the lace drapes. Damn! This was going to be a tough one. I would have to invent a story and it would have to be good.

Why, yes, Officer, I just don't know. We made mad love for five hours. I got up and went into the bathroom and when I returned, he somehow had managed to get a bullet lodged in the back of his head and splatter his brains all over Madeline's favorite set of lace drapes.

Of course, the police would suspect me and I would continue, convinced of my innocence:

Well, Officer, I just can't imagine how his blood got conveniently dabbled all over my body. Shame on these little red dots for resting on my weary flesh and bone. I can just imagine how bad this truly looks, Officer. But I swear on a stack of Louisiana Bibles, I am no more involved with this murder than I was the JFK assassination. Well, no, I cannot explain my unique set of fingerprints so beautifully placed on this frightening gun. That's just another one of life's unexplainable ironies.

And by this time the police would condemn me as crazy. But I would still go on, obsessed by this sick desire to clear my name:

Oh, now, Officer, surely you don't mean to put those unattractive cuffs around my defenseless little wrists? I just received a fresh manicure and I do believe handcuffs would certainly conflict with the feminine look I am trying so hard to achieve.

And I would laugh hysterically but at the same time hold to my stance.

Why, Officer, surely you must keep a sense of humor during a homicide investigation. If you lose your sense of humor everything else goes straight to hell. I mean, really. What are we looking at here? A dead body. Foul play. Life snuffed out in the height of its promise. A necessary phone call to soon-to-be distraught and grieving parents. And an entire family whose lives are about to be shot to hell. Shit . . . if you can't laugh it off you'd kill yourself by the end of your workday.

Silence.

You getting all of this, Officer? Why, certainly you can't expect me to humiliate myself by stepping into the back of your patrol car. Plant me on the hood and disguise me as an ornament if you have to, but whatever you do, don't put me in this steel cage in the back. If I'm riding in the back people are going to stare and I'll be so embarrassed.

The truth of it is, I was planning on having children and running for the PTA one day. But if I'm in the back of this black-and-white car with a goddamn German shepherd riding in the front, well, now, that's going to blow my PTA image straight to hell. You getting this, Officer?

So there it was, the perfect alibi. I sat myself in the backseat of my own insanity, acknowledging the only missing element of my story: *emotion.*

As I stared at Teek's dead body draped across Madeline's second-favorite bed ensemble I didn't feel the sadness commonly associated with death.

Teek was dead. Gone forever.

Didn't I love him? Didn't I care? Didn't it matter? Didn't he love me and wouldn't I miss his love? His essence? Wouldn't I wake up at night and long to touch and explore his body like I used to? *No.* And perhaps this is where sanity ends and insanity begins. I was not bothered or moved by his demise. It did not rattle my cage to swipe a damp washcloth across the lace and collect the splintered fragments of his brain. And the fact that he lay facedown in an isolated river of blood and a pile of un-invited feces didn't bother me in the least.

But how could I have taken his life with no remorse? And *did* I take his life? Well, hell, I was holding the gun. Did Audrey give me the gun? I was wearing the blood. There was nobody else in the room but the two of us, and he was dead now so I couldn't really ask him for clarification, now, could I?

When you broke it down, all you had was a dead body and a crazy, naked girl with an obligatory jail sentence, if they could prove that I did it.

And with that I contemplated a breakdown, but not before an exit to the bathroom took me away from the scene temporarily.

Upon my return to the room the blood was gone, the drapes clean, and the brain matter had been swept away. The delicate drapes hung beautifully and the bed was freshly made.

I lay my naked body back on the bed. Naked was how I liked to be. Clothing felt restrictive and confining. The largest organ in my body needed to exhale, sigh, and moan. The only time my skin crawled was when it was scrambling for breath. My flesh was so spontaneous it would shift beneath my clothes. The microscopic movement of my tissue was not radical enough to see, but it was isolated enough to feel. And it was all about enough to send me there—the other side of bonkerism, insanity, raving madness.

I felt fresh for the moment. Relieved from the pressure resting on my breasts. I had no memory of dipping myself in the tub; all I knew was that I was clean. Good—because I had other places to go. I couldn't be boggled by obsessive thoughts of my roaming, dirty skin. My problems were so much bigger than that.

And me spazzing about restless flesh at that moment was like crying over a sinking bathtub toy while the *Titanic* was dropping to the bottom of the ocean.

I could either obsess over the loss of my childhood ducky or feel compassion for the fifteen hundred people who were about to die if they didn't transform into water-breathing mammals before that flipping ship dropped below the water's surface.

I was rambling on about a boat that sank eighty years ago, dry winter skin, and a lost toy. But my energies should've been devoted to one thing: *What happened to Teek's dead body?*

Had I dragged his 230-pound frame out of the room and disposed of it? Had I made a pit stop to the store for some Mr. Clean, come back and scrubbed the room clean without knowledge of it? Had I stopped at the linen store and replaced Madeline's lace drapes? Did I get back in bed? Take a nap? Wake up? Take a shower and make the bed without skipping a beat?

"Symone, what are you looking at?" asked Teek as he emerged naked from the bathroom.

I wanted to let go of the hysteria I was courting and exchange it with a huge sigh of relief. For the first time in my life I had had a nightmare that wasn't real—or was it?

My face turned white and a chill etched my spine as I leapt from the bed and froze.

"You look like you saw a ghost," said Teek, observing my reaction.

I did see a ghost. It was lying on the bed and not just one, but two.

It was a little girl of twelve years old lying on her stomach while a naked man behind, with a crooked penis, pushed himself inside, trying to break her down, in two and in half, while squashing out her childhood dreams and extinguishing her life.

And who will tell this man that he'll scar her for but a moment now and then he'll taint her forever? Who will tell this man, *You can't do this anymore*? And who will stop this man and say, *She's just a little girl . . .*

And who will take to task to count the number of times he extracted her virginity? Who will keep track of her shattered pieces and return them when he's done? *No one*, because demons don't have eyes and mortals can't see what the hell is going on with little girls courting big intruders, trying to survive.

I stood there and watched, unable to cage the perpetrator or unglue him from the girl. His body was like twisted iron around her tiny frame. She wouldn't stand a chance now at a normal life. She would always have to fight to stay in one piece whereas others would be whole, and for that she'd hate the world. Yes, for that she'd hate the world.

I took two shallow breaths again, dying on the spot. And this is what they do—molesters kill us on the spot.

I was the ghost on the bed. A brutal flashback to life before and there never was an *after*, at least one acceptable enough to claim for decent living.

This was my childhood bedroom I was standing in.

Different furniture.

New drapes.

Fresh paint over old walls.

Updated photos.

Different flavor.

Similar feel.

Old ghosts.

Same demons.

"Teek," I whispered.

"Yeah, baby," he said.

"Go and start the car," I said, slightly away from myself. "It's time for me to leave."

"Okay," he said, nodding slowly as he if he wasn't sure. He took his time getting dressed so he could examine my every move. So I tried to sit quite still so as not to tip him off that I was a girl on the decline.

"You're coming with me, right?" he asked.

"I'll be down in a minute," I responded slowly.

"It's dark outside," he advised. "You never go out in the dark."

"Never is a long, long time . . . ," was all I said.

He nodded slowly, still observing and dissecting.

"I'll wait," he insisted.

"For what?" I asked with an edge.

"For you to get dressed and we'll walk down together."

"No," I said.

"No?" he repeated with a raised brow.

"I have to say my good-byes and . . . it's better that you just go and get the car," I snapped.

"Oh," he replied, suspicious.

Just get the hell out, Teek, I wanted to shout.

Save yourself.

Run for cover.

And don't come back again.

Can't you see the dry sperm spilled out on this floor? Many drops leaked out without a second thought. Can't you hear the sound of condoms crying out in pain? He used the rubber things with me to barricade his seed. If there had been an "accident," what would he tell his wife?

"Teek," I said, beginning to feel the strain. "Please."

"Okay," he said, still resisting. "Two minutes—I'll wait in the car two minutes, then I'm coming back in."

I nodded in agreement, giving him permission to rescue me from murder if by chance it didn't happen because I had lost my nerve.

"Two minutes," he said, holding up two fingers as if he needed to clarify what "two" really meant.

"I love you," I called out to him as he stepped beyond the door, and "Two," was all he said.

I listened to the sounds of footsteps as they carried him away. I had listened many nights for the echoing of steps because it was that hollow sound that always told my fate.

I quickly grabbed my jeans, shirt, bra, and panties, barely throwing them on in order. I stepped into my boots, then dropped to the floor, sticking my head under the bed.

I was taken aback by a sudden draft and the violent memory of being pulled from under the bed by Huston. I used to hide under the bed but it never did save me. Huston always found me, then pulled me out by both arms, kicking and clawing all the way to incest.

I had placed the gun Audrey had retrieved under this very same bed for safekeeping. I grabbed hold of it and was preparing to pull it out, load it, walk downstairs, and take him out until I was shaken by the sound of a voice.

"I forgot the keys!" said Teek, stepping around me to grab them.

Teek's return was barely a whisper but it felt like thunder to my skin. I quickly stood up, leaving the gun behind, trying to catch my breath, conceal the plan, and suppress jitters.

"What are you doing down there?" he asked suspiciously.

"Looking for spare change," I replied, so pitifully that it was obvious I was lying.

His eyes scanned the floor only to be followed by mine. And when his eyes came back to me, they searched my soul for truth. But there were no truths there, just wreckage, scar tissue, and tumor mass. I would never tell him what was beneath the bed so he would never know unless he got down on the floor and confirmed it for himself. Now, *that* would be a mistake and one he wouldn't make because he never got down on his knees. He let me be, opting instead to communicate through silence.

Don't do this, he pleaded with his eyes.

But I must, I responded to him with mine.

I won't stand by and let this happen, his body spoke.

That's why you'll wait in the car, was my final verdict sealed with a sharp turn in the opposite direction.

I stared at the walls with one lingering question: *How did I wind up here? . . . still haunted by a past that never lets me breathe.*

This was it, my life. It wasn't a perfect journey, nor a pretty one, but perhaps I should have been grateful there had even been a journey at all.

I should have abandoned the idea of killing a child molester. I should have turned my back and said, *It's time to walk away.* While Teek was standing there I should have jumped into his arms and asked to be carried away from the giant mansion and back down to the city where I could build a fence around my yard and replant all the roses. Crack down on the crack addicts and trim the weeds out back. Refinish the dining-room floor, stock up on canned goods and Kotex, marry Teek and have some babies. Take up the cello. Die old, fat, black, and happy—*this could be my life. Teek and I should make this life. I think we should take this life, take this life and run.* But when I turned around again, my baby, he was gone. And there was nothing left but silence and a wish for a different past.

CHAPTER TWENTY-FOUR

If justice would not come to me then I would go to it.

It was much too late to rescue the twelve-year-old girl on the bed who lay facedown, spread-eagle, flying over imaginary places.

When there was penetration she'd disappear and fly away. She turned into a bird and flew right by city blocks, taking in the air and the stench of morning breath. And everyone would stare in awe and wish they, too, could fly. But they would never fly like her. No, they would never fly.

Tears felt like volcano ash streaking down my cheeks. I loaded two bullets into the gun, one for his head and the other for his heart. I was optimistic about the possibility of an execution without complications because I was ill prepared to deal with anything but *smooth*.

I didn't have a plan, just a motive and a gun. And in every movie I had ever seen, that seemed to be enough. I disengaged the safety feature and then it felt so real. I opened up the door, descended down the hall, passing room after room and reliving penetration after penetration.

First I passed Audrey's room where stood the ghost of a somber girl with pretty eyes and a flair for great dramatics. But she wasn't acting out the night that he tore her way down there. He was inconsiderate and she was inconsolable when all was said and done. At least from where I stood on the other side, out here. His closing comments were made of glass cutting her: *Now, you just go to sleep.*

And then there was Chandler's room where he spent so many nights. All I heard outside her door were whimpers and pleading: "Daddy, no, please, no."

Every gruesome memory broke me down a little more until I found I was backed into a world that had no doors. I contemplated asking God's forgiveness for the killing of this man and then I remembered God and I weren't speaking anymore.

I made swift tracks down twisting stairs, heading toward the ballroom. This was an exquisite place, where all festivities were held. A crowded room pumping jazz tunes, boasting of its splendor. And the people who adorned the room were nothing extra-special, from politics to elegance, still they weren't so special. Too bad the evening guests didn't know their host was Satan.

Music and joviality crept beneath the door, and on the cusp of a victory, my feet turned to stone. I struggled to steady the gun while dripping with perspiration, standing outside the door battling a coward to step inside.

Limb to limb I shook, not knowing whether to turn, bend, yield, or run. God, I didn't want to wither but I felt myself grow weak. I knew I had to kill him now if there was ever to be peace for the little girl of yesterday who had died so long ago. And for the woman of today who was uncertain she was alive. And for all the other children who had lost their innocence before it was due to be surrendered. This could have been so beautiful had there been no complications. But there were complications.

Teek appeared from what seemed like nowhere, tackling my arm with his hands and pulling the firearm away from me, closer to him.

Don't rain on my parade! I wanted to scream, but couldn't speak. *Don't rain on my parade. Let me kill him. Let it be.*

I resisted his pull and he did the same with me. We jerked each other around in giant circles, struggling for the vibrant piece of metal.

Let the fucking gun go, it's not supposed to end this way. Teek crashed against the door and it swung open on its hinges, while the crowd looked on in horror. But not one person noticed our unannounced arrival or acknowledged the gun, which had fallen to the floor. They were all huddled in the center, removed from reality and staring at a horror all their own.

Teek grabbed the gun and held it close for safety as I slowly made my way to the center of the room where someone screamed, "Dial 911!"

911!

911!

Help!

He's down!

Call an ambulance!

We need a doctor!

Catastrophic voices were shouting out demands. What the hell was going on? I was too confused to realize and more challenged to believe that Ridge Huston was already lying on the floor. I hadn't shot him yet. No, I really hadn't shot him so why was he rehearsing for his death?

Did I shoot you by mistake? Well, if I did it was on purpose. Just thought you'd like to know the flipping truth.

"Symone," someone called, and . . .

"Symone," they said again.

"Huh?" I asked, somewhat dazed.

"Did you dial 911?" screamed Madeline. "Have you dialed 911?"

"They're coming!" screamed Chandler. "Hold on, Daddy," she said, kneeling by Huston's side. Audrey stood over them frantic and disassembled while the attorney struggled to get the crowd in check.

I was spinning around the room, in my head and not my body, grappling for knowledge I just didn't have.

"What happened?" I managed to ask one of the many guests.

"He took a real nasty spill," said an old woman with many lines upon her face.

Panic.

Sirens.

Lights and action.

Paramedics to the rescue.

They loaded Huston into the van with Madeline by his side because that's what spouses do, especially if they stand to inherit everything. Audrey and Chandler followed closely in the car, probably hoping he would change his will somewhere along the ride. And I took it all in from the window because I was too frightened of the dark to participate in theatrics, pretending that I cared.

No one had pronounced Huston dead but I sensed the Grim Reaper was not far from our block. Everyone had poured out of the house with the exception of Teek and me. And I would stay at least till sunrise, my fears would see to that.

It was 12:05 A.M. and the world had turned itself to pitch-black. I took a seat on the floor, not in the mood for conversation.

Teek stoically removed the bullets from the gun, put them in his pocket, and set the gun on the floor in front of me.

"God beat you to it," was all that he said before shunning me as he turned and walked away. His face broadcast disappointment, which was so hard to embrace. It was then I felt a shame and sanity I had never known before.

"Teek," I called out to him, but he didn't stop.

I sat there like a puppet, then I slowly came to life, finding tears from all the years I didn't cry. I was trying to survive and it simply wasn't fair, the horror of my past. The world didn't understand because the world had not been raped. It couldn't grasp the depth nor would it give me room to grieve.

The world was afraid of what had happened to me and it was easier to accept if pushed away. No one wanted to hear about the rape of a child. Details weren't ripe enough to be consumed.

Then step off if you can't handle it! I had wanted to shout so many times. Aftermath was definitely not for wimps, playing back still frames of bitter days to justify a life that made no sense.

I could hear muffled sounds of television from the other room where Teek had gone. Late-night news spilling Detroit's blues while Eden remained America's virgin city.

Yeah.

Right.

Whatever.

Teek had turned on the news to escape life with me. He was drifting far away though I could count on him to stay at least till dawn. And when the sun came up I would be on my own, my sweet love would be gone. Twisting into infinity, turning his back against me, he'd disappear like David Copperfield on crack. But I couldn't very well condemn him because I was quite a handful, and his love was pure till I tainted it with blood.

I followed the sound of boxed voices into a smaller, more cozy room. I leaned against a wall and watched Teek watch others, who felt like they were watching me. His attention was all theirs and mine was all his, humbled by the beauty of this man.

I fidgeted, shifting my weight from one hip to the other with my arms crossed. All bad-asses keep their arms crossed so I put them down, instead, by my side.

I could have pretend conversation with him, I thought, just like I did back in the day with Dolores when she was too wasted to converse. I could ask him what I wanted to know then reply with what I wanted to hear.

Do you love me?

More than I can say.

Will you stay?

Longer than you'll want me here.

Am I pretty?

"Pretty" can't describe your majesty.

Am I okay?

Sorry, no, you're not. Truthfully speaking, I believe you are insane.

Beep. Beep. Beep. Wrong answer. I couldn't even tell myself what I wanted to hear anymore.

There was nothing left to say except what we hadn't said. Teek looked so tired sitting in that chair. He looked outdone, overdone. Perhaps he had come undone with my bullshit. He wouldn't even look at me, and the vibe was so heavy that the room sulked, too.

"I'm really messed up," I said, throwing my hands in the air.

"I know," he said without emotion, staring at the television. "The minute we pulled up to this place, you turned into somebody else."

I lowered my head.

"Symone, I know you've gone through hell. You've been there, seen the shit for real . . ." He paused. "I feel your pain in my damn chest," he said, hitting his chest with his fist.

He stood up, then turned to face me. "But when is it over?" he asked, sincerely looking into my eyes. "When does the craziness stop?"

"Never," I replied, shocked that he would be rude enough to ask. "It's never over . . ."

"There are support groups out there that can help you," he said. "You're making a choice to stay in pain."

"I haven't made a real choice since the day I was born," I said, spraying bitterness from my tongue. "You ever been raped, Teek? Have you ever been turned on your back and sodomized and you couldn't do a damn thing about it—just had to lay there and take it? Do you think that was my *choice* and how I wanted to grow up?"

"No," he replied solemnly.

"You ever had somebody on top of you, pushing all of their weight onto you while they pulled your legs apart and forced you to receive them? Is that what I *chose* for this life?"

"You're not a little girl anymore . . ."

"I'm broken, don't you get it? Broken."

"When are you going to do something about it? When are you going to have a shot at a normal life?" he asked.

"Never," I replied sternly.

He reached into his pocket and pulled out the two bullets. "Then you should have used these on yourself."

Alice just got kicked out of Wonderland and Oz just burned to the ground.

"Get out!" I snapped. "Who do you think you are?"

He picked up his coat and slipped into it without protest before kissing me gently on the cheek. And this was his good-bye. I would not try to hold him because he had done his time, real time, hard time with a broken girl in foreign skin who could not get beyond her pain. I had to dismiss him because eventually I would poison him with my past and then we both would die. But if he left right now, at least one of us could be saved.

But still I struggled with it, fighting back the tears, holding down the pain, suppressing a tantrum I wanted so badly to have.

I stood there stiff, with my eyes closed because I could not bear to watch him walk away. And I didn't have the heart to ask this man to stay. Yet before his final exit he would turn to me and say, "One day, Symone, you're gonna realize that we're all victims of something."

And *poof!* Just like that he was gone, exited my life as if he had never been there at all. And there were only two things holding me back from falling out on the floor. *(1)* My jeans were too expensive to dirty; and *(2)* every good-bye ain't *gone.*

I rolled myself up into a blanket and sat in the chair Teek had just occupied, hoping to suck up his body heat. I wouldn't go to sleep, I'd simply close my eyes and wait out the night. And that was the plan, but life has a way—a funny, funny way—of rewriting your itinerary without your consent.

CHAPTER TWENTY-FIVE

Somewhere between sleep and wakefulness she came.

I was startled when I opened my eyes, only to find Madeline Huston standing over me, crowding out my space. She was waiting, lurking and contemplating. Wearing the same disguise she had always worn in a mocking attempt to pretend she was human.

She didn't say anything at first—just hovered around my chair like something from the supernatural, pale and drained of a life force. She was still wearing the same gown from the evening before, and I interpreted the unchanged wardrobe as a sign of grave preoccupation.

"He's dead," she said in a hollow voice devoid of life and also feeling. She said the words as if she had rehearsed them a thousand times before. As if she had said them in her sleep and wished them into being.

"Your father died this morning," she said in a whisper. "His heart stopped beating."

"Dead," I repeated, teetering between disbelief and jubilation. The mighty Beast had fallen. I wanted to leap from my seat and kick my heels toward the sky, but that gesture may have offended those who had loved him, if there had been any love at all. I couldn't be sure since I was unable to read Madeline's expression or the secrets of her heart to know if she was distraught, or delighted now, as I was.

"Your *father* died this morning," she repeated somewhat gone, somewhat here.

"I understand," I said softly.

"Your father died this morning," she said again.

Perhaps she had gone mad and maybe that was why she kept repeating herself. "I don't think you heard me . . . ," she insisted.

"I heard you," I said, trying to suffocate my annoyance.

"Symone," said Madeline, flustered and compressed, "Ridge was your biological father," she blurted, shattering me with news so hard it stung.

"No," I heard myself cry out, and the image of what I had thought I was spilled out onto the floor—so much for "choices."

"Ridge had an affair with your mother while on one of his many business trips," she explained. "His indiscretions were tiresome," she said with exhaustion. "After your mother died he felt compelled to bring you here once he learned of your existence," she said with a hint of bitterness.

I was stunned.

Numb.

Confused.

Nothing like an eleventh-hour kick below the belt and into the groin, blowing you to pieces. I felt like a zombie, unsure how to respond, barely there, with my guts splattered all about the floor. Life was writing me into *its* story, scripting the dialogue, blocking the moves. I was only there to act out what had been written on the page; a puppet without a voice speaking wordless words to deaf ears. I was a song devoid of notes but somehow I was still being played.

"What are you saying?" I asked as I jumped from my seat and also from my skin. "It can't be! My mother never knew Ridge Huston!" I was defensive, in search of an alternative biological explanation.

"She knew him well enough to give him a child," she said, spraying me with resentment. "*And* to put his name on your birth certificate which is how the state of Massachusetts tracked us down after your mother died. Shattered my life to hell the day I got the call," she said quietly.

"My mother struggled like a dog to take care of me when I was little. Why didn't she get child support from him if I was really his child?" I asked, challenging her theory. "Why didn't she make him pay?"

"Symone," said Madeline, shaking her head. "She did make him pay. He paid dearly."

There was a lot to read in between the pauses, gaps, and the sighs. Huston had gotten Dolores pregnant and then he disappeared before knowing he fathered a bastard child. And this worked out conveniently for Huston because the locals wouldn't have appreciated the truth anyway. But life exposed his indiscretion when it showed up on the Hustons' doorstep as a little, black, orphan child.

"It destroyed our family," Madeline mumbled. "We had to rebuild our lives the best we could. Audrey and Chandler don't even know the truth to this day."

"Is that why?" I asked.

"Why what?" she asked.

"Is that why you brought me here?" I asked with tears in my eyes. I asked *"Why?"* because I wanted to know. I asked "Why?" because answers were necessary, urgent, and long overdue. Not only did I wish to know why the Hustons had brought me here but I also wanted to know *why* Ridge ravaged his girls? What fueled the Beast in his bidding for the devil? And how did Madeline allow this all to happen? She was an advocate of the abuse because she didn't prevent it from occurring *again* and *again*. I looked into her eyes with contempt because her absence left the gap wide open for entry of the Beast. And it wasn't that she was absent, she was there—she just wasn't really *there*, you know? She made a showing in the physical form with a light hand stretched outward awaiting a heavy cash deposit. She always showed up to show off her shit. To make an entrance in fur coats, fine diamonds, and extraordinary apparel. To engage in frivolous gossip at afternoon tea parties about the neighbors and their business, shortcomings, and dysfunction. But never to explain her position and expose the wailing demons that lived just beneath the gates of her own palace. Madeline had all of the answers to everyone's problems and everyone's saga but her own. She spent her entire life worrying about looking good and not a moment did she place herself on pause in pursuit of actually *being* good.

So again I asked her "Why?" and again I met her silence. Perhaps silence was the only answer she was capable of providing because in the end there were no answers, except the one she told herself so as to get to sleep each night. And the one she would eventually spill to me:

"We brought you here because your mother was dead and to walk away and leave you in an orphanage would have made us *animals* . . . don't you think?" she asked with one raised brow. She smiled a peculiar smile and then she walked away. And with that I understood how the Beast had found his mate, for at the core they were the same and so deserving of each other in every way.

CHAPTER TWENTY-SIX

I disappeared inside of myself, absorbing the knowledge that he was my father much like the ocean recedes to make room for the waves.

We blend to become one with the complexities of life, carrying within us the good seeds and the bad. We bleed into our truths until we become immune to them and then we just go numb.

Ridge Huston was buried in an elaborate ceremony five days later. It was at his funeral I realized that every time someone dies, it is we, the living, who shift to fill in the empty holes. And once the entire world has shifted, it is almost as if the dead had never lived at all. And that was the only comfort that made it almost bearable. For we shift without the knowledge that we have even moved an inch, giving credence to the adage, *Life must go on.*

It's ironic how the dead can be forgotten once the sting of their departure wears off. Most will barely remember Ridge Huston in the years to come, but Audrey, Chandler, and I, we won't forget. We were all recipients of his cryptic tattoo, one that branded us as Huston girls for life.

Six months after Ridge's passing, life returned to normal, or as normal as it would ever be. Madeline grieved in her own subtle way, where she mourned the loss of his role more than the loss of his life. And she would miss having a husband more than she enjoyed being a wife. And in her greatest sorrow I truly do believe that the only thing she missed was the *familiar*.

Madeline inherited the Huston fortune and distributed fair portions among Audrey, Chandler, and even me, the bastard child. She also relinquished control of the gallery and returned the rights to me. I was impressed by this display; however, I still judged her harshly. I had always tolerated her in the dubious role of stepmother and the more I learned of her, the less it all made sense. My opinion of her was comparable to my passion for her, rare and fleeting. And if I thought anything at all of her, it would have been irrigated by disapproval because of her inability to rescue us as children.

A parent's job is to protect their children from evil, even if that evil is the other parent. Good parents don't let giant monsters slip through the cracks without their eventual capture and detainment.

In my heart I will always believe Madeline *knew* of the horrors we suffered as children. And so, too, I also believed it was residual guilt that served as the foundation for the pay out (reading between the lines: *pay off*) upon the passing of the Beast. Why else would Madeline have been so gracious with the inheritance when it was not in her nature to be unselfish at all?

This was pure speculation unsubstantiated by facts but I have learned along my journey's way, in the homes we are born in, live in, and die in, there are very few *real* surprises. No one gets away with the violent abuse of a child without the consent of a silent partner. And that exposition was the kindest manner in which I could quantify my summation: *The evil bitch knew what was going on in her own damn house.*

And as for Audrey, she grieved for her father less quietly than Madeline and was prone in the early days to shed many tears. And hysterics and theatrics—drama, more drama because that was how dear Audrey lived. She never spoke of the abuse again and it had vanished when she wished it away, suppressing on impact the push of the past so the pain never managed to stay, at least on the surface where others could see it. It was easier for Audrey to live in a world where the rape never happened than to reside in the one where it did.

Audrey made a living doing what she did best. She became an Eden socialite and took up the good life on a full-time basis. She toured around the city, a spokesperson for the Huston legacy, holding up her father's image in high regard to the public because that was what a *good* Huston did.

She surrounded herself with beautiful things and gorgeous people, because that was her gift, making life look pretty. I came to realize that not every living creature was filled with heavy purpose. And as for Audrey, she was one of those creatures.

One day she would probably marry a wealthy man and they would raise a handsome family. She would continue to be consumed with the making of a life*style* and overlook the making of a *life*. But it really wouldn't matter just as long as her life was a courtship of all that was pretty.

Chandler adjusted quickly upon the passing of Ridge. At least that's what she reflected from the outside in, lest we all be fooled by appearance. She shed four tears at the funeral, and I know because I counted, and then her grief seemed to disappear. Not that it actually *vanished*, but perhaps it just changed form.

Chandler took up hobbies like being a martyr and a caretaker, enlisting her services to fight for everybody's cause.

The broken.
The battered.
The solemn.
The blue.
Chandler's the girl.
Fighting for you.

She devoted her life to the service of others in Detroit's inner city where she set out to change the world. *Somebody* had to do it. Save the environment by closing the hole in the earth's ozone layer. Prevent the overpopulation of cats, dogs, and rodents.

I admired her heart for being so grand but I also felt there were motives. Saving others is a way of redeeming oneself without saying out loud, *I, too, have problems.*

Chandler never shed the weight, only the concept of being thin, and perhaps this was the way she managed to stay sane. She, too, would never mention the rape again; instead she buried it in the intricacies of one-woman crusades and also underneath the layers of her skin.

Through Audrey and Chandler, I learned that everyone does survival differently. And I was in no position to judge the manner in which they chose to stay afloat.

Teek disappeared in the fashion of Houdini, assigning "loneliness" to lead all of my dances.

And me—what of me, the ultimate train wreck... What would become of my life? I didn't mourn the way ordinary children grieved dead parents, because I was a stranger to *ordinary*.

Huston's death brought me peace and I was relieved in many ways that he was gone. The world would never be large enough to house his body and my pain in the same sphere. And though I had consumed myself with thoughts of the killing of a child molester, I was grateful his final chapter had not been written with my blood. Hence the birth of a miracle child, and I called her "*second chances.*"

Would I excavate the courage to fight for my life when it was easier to bend toward madness? Would I feel my way through the pain when it was easier to numb it with hate? Would I find a life of choices and deny a life of fate? Would I walk through the flames instead of standing in the fire, petitioning the crowd by playing victim to the hilt? I was so damn good at the part. The part of the broken, the part of the bruised, the part of the shattered, the part of the used. Out of all the king's horses and all the king's men, who would put Symone back together again?

Six months and one day following the death of Ridge Huston, I entered recovery. I joined an incest survivors' group and sought life beyond where the road runs out.

I attended biweekly meetings in simple rooms of complex worlds where I was introduced to people who were just like me, broken dolls on the mend authenticating the definition of courage.

Olivia taught me courage when she stood up and shared that she had been raped by an uncle. And Maya taught me courage when she broke the silence of rape at the hands of her brother. Annette taught me courage when she spoke out against the rape committed by her pastor. And twins Derek and Dillon taught me courage when they stood up and shared the sins of their father and uncle. And on and on went the twisted tales of sexual dysfunction, graphic violence, and ritualistic abuse. These adult children were so damaged, so bruised, that I marveled to see they were still aboveground. Every new horror tipped the scales more outrageously than the last. Some of the stories were so unforgivable that it appeared my life had been *easy*.

The rooms bled together and the rooms cried together and the rooms healed together in due time. And within these simple rooms I found my redemption and began to understand I had a *choice*. I was more than the past that had delivered me here, and more than the pain that defined me. Indeed, I was a rare and beautiful bird from the species known as *survivor*.